THE SECRET OF SOMERSET PLACE

Written and Photographed
by
Carole Marsh

Published by Gallopade Publishing Group
Rocky Mount & Tryon, North Carolina

Copyright © 1980 by Carole Marsh

All rights reserved. No part of this book may be reproduced or copied in any form without written permission of the publisher. For information contact Gallopade Publishing Group, P.O. Box 469, Rocky Mount, North Carolina 27801.

Published by Gallopade Publishing Group. Printed in the United States of America by Faith Printing Company, Taylors, S.C.

Cover design by Carole Marsh and Rich Haynes. Map by Marion Weathers.

Library of Congress Card Number: 80-84084
ISBN: 0-935326-02-2

Although Somerset Place and Lake Phelps are real places, all characters and events in this book are purely fictional and bear no intentional resemblance to living persons or actual occurrences.

About the Book . . .

"They call this place the *Haunt of Beasts,*" said Wendy Long, age twelve.

"This place" was Somerset — a coastal plantation in eastern North Carolina, near Lake Phelps — one of the most remote areas in the South.

No one believed there were still beasts — not until an important report that would affect the future of the lake disappeared. Next, clues appeared, sending the characters on a beast-hunting chase through the historic house and grounds.

A little luck and a little reading on the history of Somerset helps Wendy and her friends understand why the plantation way of life vanished; what ecological succession is; the value of historic preservation; and why they still do call Somerset "the haunt of beasts."

By the time the resourceful children solve "The Secret of Somerset Place," you'll be a believer — in a bad, old beast and a good, new book!

Dedication

This book is dedicated to the "real" Wendy, Marc, Wanda, and Michael.

Table of Contents

1. The Haunt of Beasts........................1
2. There Is a Beast!..........................7
3. The Great Alligator Dismal Swamp..........13
4. A Face in the Window......................19
5. Easter Morning Mystery....................27
6. A Slippery, Wet Clue......................35
7. The Lost Lake.............................41
8. A Scare on Finder's Island................49
9. The Little Attic Room.....................55
10. Did They Drown?...........................63
11. The Ooey, Gooey Clue......................71
12. A Mortal Fever............................77
13. A Mysterious Moan.........................83
14. A Blue Clue...............................87
15. Rich Lands................................91
16. The Bad, Old Beast........................97
17. A Weird Wedding..........................103
18. Help!....................................109

19 A Chase Through the Swamp..............113
20 Bless the Beast..........................117

1 The Haunt of Beasts

"They call this place the *haunt of beasts,*" Wendy said.

Michael's scrawny legs hung over the edge of the porch. He swung them back and forth a few times before he answered. "I don't believe in beasts," he finally said, cocking his big blue eyes up at the other kids to see if they believed him.

"She's not kidding," Marc assured Michael, rocking the porch swing slowly back and forth. "You can see how lonesome this place is."

"And this place gets real spooky at night," said Wanda from the porch steps.

This place — Somerset Place — Wendy thought, gazing out across the yard to the lake. It was just as flat as a desert, but everything was as green and lush as a jungle.

Even now, Somerset Place was one of the most remote areas in North Carolina. And this was where she — a twelve-year-old girl from the big city of Atlanta — was just dying to live.

"I know you're eleven, Marc Walker, but you'd be scared yourself if you ever saw a beast," Wendy said. "But not me — I'm ready to live with beasts!"

Wendy's Uncle Ed was going to buy some land on the other side of Lake Phelps — or the haunt of beasts — as she liked to call it. He was the overseer of Somerset Place, the big, old plantation beside the lake.

They let him live in this small Gate House. But when he and Wendy moved, they would have their own house and a boat dock. Uncle Ed had promised Wendy that she could get her horse, Charley, out of boarding and bring it here.

"Where's your uncle going to build his house?" Wanda asked.

Wendy slung her brown hair back and thrust an arm up in dismay. *"Build the house?* He can't even buy the land until everything's decided about the lake!"

"What's to decide?" Michael asked, staring out at Lake Phelps, puzzled. "It isn't going anywhere, is it?"

Marc stopped the swing. "As a matter of fact, it is," he said. "It's going up and down. My Dad says the environmental people want to get the lake to one level and keep it there."

Wendy frowned. Marc was a real bookworm. He was always trying to show off how smart he was, she thought. His dad was the superintendent of Pettigrew State Park and so Marc thought that made him an expert about Somerset Place.

"So why don't they just do it?" Wendy said, sliding off of the porch rail.

"That's not as easy as it sounds," Marc explained.

"Dad says if they fill it too high, the homeowners on the opposite shore of the lake won't be able to use their septic tanks. And if they keep it too low, the fishermen complain."

"My mama says they ought to leave the lake to nature and not mess with it at all," Wanda said. She was nine. Her mother was the housekeeper of the plantation.

"Your mama's crazy," Marc grumbled. "Nature needs all the help it can get these days, the way people take advantage of it."

"My mama knows more than you think," Wanda protested. "She's seen the lake almost up to The Big House before."

Holding onto the banisters, Michael stretched back and looked up at The Gate House.

"Not The Gate House," Wendy said. "The Big House."

They all turned toward the plantation by the lake. Josiah Collins the third, or Joe 3, as Marc called him, had built the mansion around 1830. He named it Somerset Place after his family home in England. The mansion had been restored. Smart-alec Marc had told her that meant they fixed it back as close as possible to the way it was when the Collinses lived here.

It looked like a gigantic, pale yellow cake sitting in the grass. A homemade cake for sure, Wendy thought, because the three stories were like lopsided layers where the house had settled with age in the soft, swampy ground.

"Who lives in The Big House?" Michael asked. He had come to Somerset to stay during Easter vacation. His mother was a friend of Uncle Ed's. She was on the

Outer Banks finishing a book of histories about the coastal towns there. And his sister, Michele, was in Bath rehearsing to be in the Blackbeard the Pirate play this summer.

Wendy thought Michael had that homesick look she used to get after her mother died and she had moved to Grandmother's. He was only eight, and this was a weird, lonesome place to spend a vacation.

"No one lives there now," she told Michael, sitting down beside him. Her legs would barely fit under the skinny bottom rail of the porch. She decided jogging by the lake must be building up her leg muscles pretty good.

"It was once a big plantation," she added. "The Collins family lived there and they grew all kinds of crops around here, even rice."

"Sounds like a lot of hard work," Michael said, sprawling lazily out on the cool boards of the porch floor.

"They had a lot of help," said Marc.

"Yes, *a lot,*" Wanda agreed with a frown.

Wendy looked at her understandingly. She was one of the cutest girls she knew. She had a pretty smile and big brown eyes.

"They couldn't have farmed as much as they did if it hadn't been for . . ." Wendy began.

" . . . For the slaves," Marc interrupted.

It seemed strange to Wendy to think of Wanda's ancestors as being slaves. She couldn't imagine being owned by someone else — someone who could boss you around all they wanted to. That's bad enough when you're a kid, she thought. But when you're an adult, that would be miserable.

She wondered how the Collins family and their slaves had liked living at the haunt of beasts. Wendy lived in Atlanta now. But Grandmother had said that if Uncle Ed built a house by the end of summer, she could live at Somerset the coming school year.

Wendy loved the outdoors, especially boating and swimming and fishing and sailing and water skiing. She had lived in a big apartment building in downtown Atlanta for two years, and that was enough. The apartment manager fussed when she turned cartwheels down the long halls of the building. And there was no place to swim. (She had tried the fountain in front of the apartment when she thought no one was looking. The manager complained to Grandmother that time.)

Everyone agreed that it would be best if she came to live at Somerset Place with Uncle Ed. *If* he could get a house of his own. Grandmother didn't want Wendy to live in the overseer's house with so many strangers in and out. You get cautious about things like that when you live in a big city.

Somerset sure wasn't the big city. It wasn't even a little town. Grandmother would call it the *boondocks*, for sure. That meant it was out in nowhere.

Poor Grandmother! She said it tired her out to keep up with a girl who tried so hard to live up to her name. Grandmother always swore that Wendy blew in one door and out the other. Never walked; always ran. She even smiled fast.

If you would just put as much energy into your schoolwork, Grandmother would always say. She had even made Wendy promise to read for one hour every day if she came to Somerset for Easter vacation. And boy, was Uncle Ed making her live up to that bargain!

An owl hooted. "Oh, that's just Captain Horniblow," Wanda said.

It was starting to get dark. Michael looked more miserable than ever. "It *is* spooky out here," he said.

"Don't worry," Wendy assured him. "We can explore the lake. The Easter picnic's tomorrow and Mr. Snoad, the real estate agent, is having a big wedding next Sunday. Maybe he will take us over in his boat to see the property Uncle Ed's going to buy," she added eagerly.

"And you can come up to The Big House and see me," Wanda added. "Mama's always baking something good to eat."

Michael's blue eyes brightened at that offer.

"And if you get lonesome at night," Marc said slowly, in a deep, spooky voice, "there's always the beast to keep you company."

Wendy glared at him. He was too big to try and scare Michael like that, she thought. Just as she started to tell him off, Uncle Ed came storming out onto the porch. He stared at them all with wide, wild eyes that were the same color as the gray lake.

Wendy had never seen him look that way. "What's wrong?" she asked urgently.

He looked blankly at her, then slowly lifted his long arm and pointed a bony finger toward the lake.

"The beast," he said. *"The beast!"*

2 There Is a Beast!

All the kids jumped up. "What beast?!" they squealed together.

Uncle Ed stumbled over to the porch swing and slumped down. His gray hair stood out in all directions like shocks of swamp grass. A porcupine stubble of beard covered the bottom half of his face. His eyes darted back and forth in confusion. Wendy thought he looked a little like a beast himself.

She sat down on the porch swing beside him and took his hand. "What beast?" she repeated gently.

He looked at her and the others as though he had just really seen them. "Some beast has stolen the environmental impact report," he said.

Everyone looked puzzled except Marc. "You mean the report on the lake water level my dad did?" he asked.

Uncle Ed nodded his head and Marc let out a long, slow whistle.

"Your dad brought it over to me yesterday afternoon," Uncle Ed said. "I left it on my desk last night. And now, it's gone . . . vanished."

Wendy didn't understand what was such a big deal about a bunch of papers. It sounded too much like schoolwork to her. "So what?" she said.

Uncle Ed frowned at her. "So we can't buy the property and build a house unless that report is found."

Wendy's mouth flew open. "Why not?" she demanded.

"They won't release any of the waterfront land to buyers until the decision is made on what level to keep the lake," Uncle Ed explained.

"And the information in that report is what they were going to base the decision on," Marc added.

"Can't they just do the report over?" Wanda asked hopefully.

Marc shook his head. "It took Dad six months of research and tests to come up with the figures. They were going to review the report and decide what to do about the lake soon."

"And we were supposed to buy our lot right after that," Uncle Ed added sourly.

"Don't you have another copy of the report?" Michael asked. "My mother's a writer and she makes copies of everything — even my report cards," he added with a frown.

"That's what I was going to do today," Uncle Ed said. "That was the only copy and now someone has stolen it."

Wendy sank back against the swing. The skinny slats mashed into her backbone. They had to be kidding, she thought. It was just a bunch of papers. How could they make her miss getting to live at Somerset Place. They just couldn't!

She jumped up out of the swing and paced back and forth across the long, narrow porch. "Who would steal the report?" she asked.

"A lot of people don't want the level changed," her uncle said. He had settled down and didn't look so wild-eyed. "Some want it kept high; others want it kept low."

"My mama says . . ." Wanda began.

"*Everybody* says something different," Marc interrupted.

"Well, wouldn't we lose part of the land we want to buy if they raise the water level?" Wendy asked, sinking back down in the swing.

"Yes," Uncle Ed answered. "And we would have to sign a paper saying we would still buy the property. But I don't care. I guess others might use that as an excuse to back out of a deal. But what's best for the lake is fine with me."

Suddenly Uncle Ed jumped up from the porch swing, sending Wendy on a jiggled, twist-turn ride. "Marc — you go tell your dad what's happened," he ordered. "Wanda, you go ask your mama if she's seen anyone strange hanging around."

"Are we looking for a beast?" Michael asked, not budging from his grip on the banisters.

Uncle Ed frowned. "I'm afraid that the beast we're looking for has two legs and a head full of mean ideas about how to mess up other people's business."

He looked at Wendy sadly. "If we don't find that report, we won't get to build our house before school starts," he said. "You and Michael walk around and see if you see anything suspicious. *NOW!*" he added with a snap of his fingers.

They all jumped as though a real beast had startled them.

Marc scrambled down the porch steps and hurried toward the Pettigrew State Park office next door.

"Yes sir!" Wanda said, scurrying toward The Big House crying, "Mama! Mama!"

Michael scooted out of his perch under the banisters. Wendy bounded right over the porch rail onto the ground. "Let's look around The Village," she said.

Michael slapped his skinny arms against his sides. "Where is it?" he asked.

Wendy waved her arm to cover the entire area around The Gate House. "Right here!" she said. "All of these small buildings were part of the Somerset plantation. Visitors said it looked like a village. So, that's what everyone still calls it."

Single-file, they walked up and down the narrow brick sidewalks that criss-crossed through The Village. Wendy called off the names of the small buildings as they passed them — "the dairy . . . the kitchen . . . woodhouse . . . bath house . . ."

She stopped in front of two tiny, pointed-roof buildings. "And these are the privies," Wendy said, trying not to smile. "Do you know what that is?"

Michael grinned. "Yeah! They're outdoor bathrooms. Michele already tricked me about that when we were in Bath last summer," he said, his cheeks turning pink.

Wendy laughed and they walked toward The Big House. It was three stories high with open porches all around and lots of tall windows to catch the breezes off the lake.

The front porch did not face the lake, but a big grassy area with a circle of huge oak trees around it. "They call this The Great Lawn," Wendy said. "They used to have horse races here. And they're going to have races on Mr. Snoad's wedding day."

"Does this river go to the lake?" Michael asked, pointing to the narrow strip of water that ran between the house and The Lawn.

Wendy laughed again. "That's not a river," she said. "This is just one of a bunch of canals that go into the lake."

"Uncle Ed says that the lake is higher than the land," she explained. "So Mr. Collins — Joe 3 — figured out that if they dug some canals, the water would flow out of the lake by gravity. Then they could use it to irrigate their crops."

"Like pulling the bathtub plug?" Michael said.

"Sort of," Wendy said. "And the plug is the watergate at the end of each canal."

Michael stared down the long stretch of canal. "Someone dug these things?" he asked in amazement.

"The slaves that Joe 3 brought from Africa did," Wendy said. *"One hundred and thirty* miles of canals," she added.

"Wow!" Michael exclaimed, stepping closer to the edge of the water.

"Be careful," Wendy warned. "Uncle Ed says the canals are pretty deep and when the water is moving fast, it could sweep you away."

Michael stepped back and Wendy sighed. "Well, I don't see anything unusual around here," she said.

"Let's go over to the Pettigrew Place and look around. I've never been over there anyway."

A dirt bridge over the canal changed into a spooky, overgrown path that led away from The Lawn. Wendy crossed first and Michael followed.

"What is the Pettigrew Place?" Michael asked, ducking under a drooping vine.

Wendy stepped over a bunch of briars. "There's not anything left of it now, but it was the homeplace of another family that lived near the lake when the Collinses did."

"It's almost dark," Michael said. "Do we have to go down there?"

Wendy peered down the dark path of snaky vines and skeletal tree branches that grabbed hands overhead. She didn't want to admit that Uncle Ed had told her not to go to the Pettigrew Place.

"Well, if I were a beast or a thief, this looks like the kind of place I might go and hide," Wendy said. "And I really need to find that report," she added.

They plodded on. The path grew thicker. It was almost dark in the leafy green tunnel.

"Yes," said Wendy, slowing her steps. "If I had stolen something and wanted to hide, this would be the place. And I'm not afraid," she said, but softly as though she were trying to convince herself even more than Michael. "I'm not afraid of any old beast . . ."

Just as she said the word *beast* — she and Michael stopped dead in their tracks and screamed.

3 The Great Alligator Dismal Swamp

"A beast!" they screamed together. They turned and ran as fast as they could back to the canal.

At the dirt bridge, Wendy tripped and Michael tumbled over her like they were playing leap frog.

"Did you see it?" she cried, gripping his shoulders so tightly he squealed again.

"Y-yes," he stammered. "There really is a beast!"

They both stood very still staring into the tunnel.

"We'd better go tell Uncle Ed," Wendy said, starting to run again. "I know he said a beast stole the lake level report. And I know he was only kidding, but . . ."

The rest of her words were lost in the wind. She was running so fast she could hardly breathe. She thought Uncle Ed and Marc were only kidding about there being beasts — real beasts — around Somerset Place. She wondered if they would be surprised to hear about this one.

Poor Michael! He thought he was going to have a

Finder's Island

Lake Phelps

Wood House

The Gate House

Wash House

Dairy

Ice House

Kitchen

"The Big House"

Kitchen Stores

Smoke House

Garden

road

to Rich Lands

"The Great Lawn"

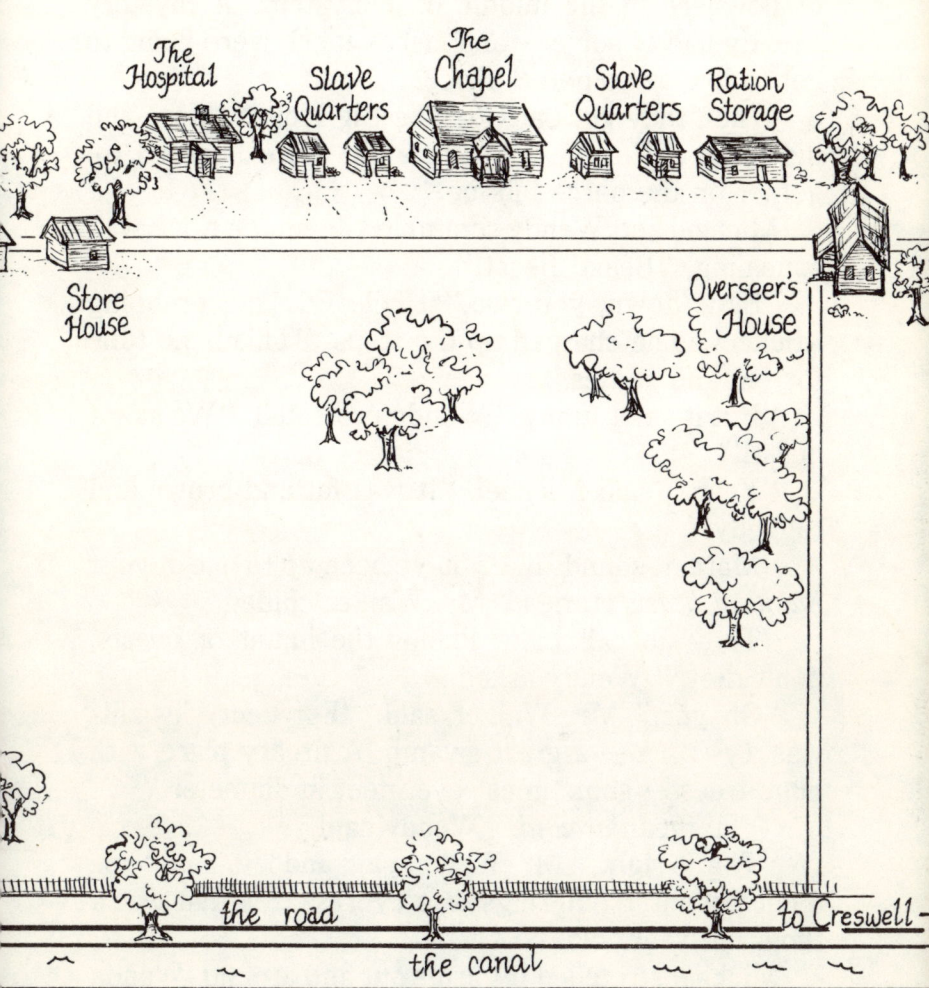

quiet Easter vacation. And now he was in the middle of nowhere in the middle of a mystery. A mystery Wendy had to solve — and fast — if she were going to get to live at Somerset Place.

When they got back to The Big House, Marc and his father, Wanda, and Uncle Ed were huddled together on the porch talking.

Michael and Wendy scrambled down the brick wall squealing, "Beast! Beast!"

"Slow down, you two," Uncle Ed said, grabbing Michael as he charged up the steps. "This is no time for fun and games."

"But it's not funny," Wendy protested. "We saw a beast!"

"Yeah," said Michael. "It was fat and brown and raggedy."

"Marc, it sounds like you've been up to one of your *haunt of beasts* stories," Mr. Walker chided.

"They do call Lake Phelps the haunt of beasts, don't they?" Wendy asked.

"Oh yes," Mr. Walker said. "For centuries this was a *pocosen* — a great swamp. A dreary place with huge trees — sometimes seven feet in diameter."

"You mean *around?*" Wendy said.

"That's right," Mr. Walker said and laughed. "Joe 3 once counted 800 rings on a cypress tree that was a thousand years old."

Michael stretched his arms out and around. Wanda giggled and put her arms out to meet his.

"Bigger than that!" Uncle Ed said.

Marc and Wendy joined hands with the others and made a circle, stretching to barely touch fingertips.

"That's more like it," Mr. Walker said.

"Wow!" said Michael.

"What about the beasts?" Wanda asked.

"Oh, there were bears and wolves," Mr. Walker said.

Wanda wrapped her arms around her shoulders and shivered.

"Panthers . . . wildcats," Mr. Walker went on. "Rattlesnakes . . . and gigantic bullfrogs."

"Are the beasts still here?" Wendy asked.

Mr. Walker nodded his head *yes*. "The whole area had been considered worthless. On old maps it was labeled The Great Alligator Dismal Swamp," he said. "It was so thick and fearsome that explorers could not even enter the area and regarded it as nothing but a haunt of beasts."

"So, we did see a beast," Wendy pleaded, stomping her foot. She didn't like being half-scared out of her wits only to have a bunch of adults and a smart-alec boy not believe her.

"It was something . . . or someone, wasn't it, Michael?" she added.

Michael's round white face bobbed up and down like a marshmallow.

"Well, whatever you saw," Uncle Ed said, "I doubt it has anything to do with the disappearance of the lake level report. The beast who stole that is bound to be human."

"And unfortunately, there's so much disagreement about the lake that it could be just about anyone," Mr. Walker grumbled.

Wanda's mother, Mrs. Sawyer (she pronounced it *Mizriz)* waddled down the brick walk toward them. "Ought to leave that lake to nature," she argued.

"See what Dad means?" Marc hissed.

"Well, it doesn't matter, now," Uncle Ed said. "We've got a lot to do to prepare for the Easter festivities tomorrow, so let's get at that."

The thought of Easter day made Wendy feel better. They were going to have a sunrise service by the lake, an Easter egg hunt, and a big breakfast picnic under the cypress trees. Michael's mother and sister were coming, which Wendy knew would make Michael happy. Of course, it might not make his mother happy to hear he'd seen a beast, Wendy thought.

Last summer his sister, Michele, had solved a spooky mystery of a missing prop pirate head from the outdoor drama in Bath. Maybe she could give Wendy some clues to solving this mystery.

Clues, Wendy thought, that's what we need. The thief — beast or not — had to leave some kind of a clue somewhere. Didn't it?

"Let's pick up some of the fallen limbs by the lake before dark," Mr. Walker said.

"Aw, let's wait for a swamp fire," Marc grumbled.

"What's that?" Wendy asked.

"When they would clear land and burn stumps, the wind would stir up the ashes and burn the peat on the ground by the lake," Mr. Walker explained. "In fact, it's believed that a natural fire that burned a deep hollow that filled with black swamp water is how Lake Phelps was formed."

He and Marc headed toward the lake.

"I'm making zuzus," Mizriz Sawyer announced. "You chirrun want to help?"

Chirrun was what she called children. Zuzus were an old-fashioned kind of gingersnap cookie. Wanda's mother's were delicious. The rich molasses she used made them just as dark as she was. Hot from the oven with a cold glass of milk — what a bedtime snack!

"Yummy!" Wendy cried. "We'll help."

She glanced at Uncle Ed for his approval. He just nodded. She knew his mind was still on the stolen report. Wendy wanted to tell him not to worry, that she was going to solve that mystery just as fast as she could so he could buy his property and start their new house. But she decided that would just worry him even more.

Wendy leaned over the edge of the porch rail and looked across the canal. Where was the beast now, she wondered. And where had it come from?

And then a thought came to her that gave her chills even on this warm spring night. *Would the beast come back?*

4 A Face in the Window

Wendy sighed. Wanda had taken Michael in The Big House to show him around. She hurried to join them for a quick tour while Mizriz Sawyer got out the ingredients for the cookies.

She pushed the big front door open. Michael was standing in the huge hall, his eyes wide. "You mean people really used to live in this big, old house?" he asked.

Wendy knew that he lived in an apartment too and would think the house was as gigantic as she did. "Sure," she said, closing the heavy front door behind her. "The Collins family had two sons about your age. Uncle Ed said they came here from New York."

She smiled to think of how different that must have been. A *culture shock* Grandmother would say.

"Is the house haunted?" Michael asked, looking at the curved steps that led to the second floor.

"Mama and I have never seen a ghost," Wanda

said. "But . . ."

Suddenly there was a tap-tap behind them on a window pane beside the front door. They gasped and swung around.

A face in the window stared at them. It was Marc. "Let me in," he called.

Wanda tugged the heavy door open again.

"You scared us to death!" Wendy said.

"By knocking on the front door?" Marc asked in mock surprise.

"We were talking about ghosts," Michael explained.

Marc grinned, "I know."

"And I was just going to tell them about . . ." Wanda began, when they heard a call from the parlor.

"Stop that rumpus in the hall," Mizriz Sawyer called. "Anyone wanting zuzus for Easter — and maybe before —" she hinted, "better get themselves in my kitchen."

Everyone except Wendy bounded through the library to head for the kitchen building.

"Wait!" Wendy protested, but found she was talking to an empty hall. Brother, she thought. With all these interruptions she was never going to solve this mystery. She wished she knew more about the house, especially about what Wanda just was going to tell them.

Her uncle always said that if she would read more she would know more. As she passed through the library she stopped to look at the books stacked sleepily against one another in their glass case. She figured she would have to spend some time reading about the history of Somerset Place.

She knew Marc knew a lot about the Lake Phelps area. Half the time she saw him, he was sitting under one of the gigantic cypress trees reading. But he was so smart-alecky about what he knew that she hated to ask him anything. He was too eager to tell her *everything* he knew — which was usually about a lakeful more than what she wanted to know.

Suddenly, Wendy realized she was alone in the house. Everything was still and quiet. Moonlight danced on the library wall. Through the rippled panes of old glass, it made ghostly shadows on the wall.

Wendy hurried into a smaller room and then into a hall. She sure didn't like parading around this house at night by herself. "Wanda," she said softly, but her voice was lost in the huge house. "Marc?" she called louder. The only answer was the echo of her own voice.

Again there was a tap-tap-tap behind her. Startled, she turned.

Marc poked his head in the side door and grinned. "It's not a ghost," he said and giggled.

"Cut that out!" Wendy said. "You keep sneaking up like that on purpose!"

"No, I don't," Marc protested. "Mizriz Sawyer sent me to see if you got lost," he said grumpily, "but if you want to stay over here by yourself . . ." he added, storming out and slamming the door.

"No, wait!" she called, following him. "I'm sorry," she said. "This place just makes you jumpy when you're by yourself."

Marc stopped and looked back. "It is a big, old, rambling place, isn't it? And you should see the attic!"

"The attic?"

"Sure. It's at the top of a little flight of stairs off the second floor," he began, as they walked toward the kitchen.

Mizriz Sawyer poked her head out of the kitchen building door. "Stop your long-winded harangue and get in here," she called.

"She means *hush,*" Marc said, hurrying inside.

Phooey, Wendy thought. It was going to be Christmas instead of Easter before she found the report. And there wasn't any time to waste. Oh well, she thought, every beast hunter needs energy, so she might as well give in and eat some cookies.

The kitchen was in a separate small brick house away from the mansion. Mizriz Sawyer hovered over a big earthen bowl.

Wendy thought how many slaves it must have taken to run the household when the Collinses lived here. Why, some had probably spent most of their lives in this kitchen. She imagined how sweltering hot it must have gotten in the summer when all the big brick ovens were fired up to prepare dinner for the hundreds of people who lived in The Village.

But now the kitchen was cool, thanks to a window air conditioner Uncle Ed had installed. A fine mist of flour and cinnamon wafted through the air.

Marc, Wanda and Michael concentrated on pushing long-handled wooden spoons through the thick, dark batter. Mizriz Sawyer bounced from one bowl to the other adding some molasses from a jar here, and sampling a taste of batter with her little finger there.

"Are we making cookies for the whole world?" Wendy teased.

"Got to have a lot for the Easter celebration," Mizriz Sawyer said, grabbing a spoon. "Besides, I still like to cook like my grandma did for the Collinses — in *great stile,*" she said.

She stopped stirring, her spoon frozen in the batter. "The Collinses were rich as molasses," she said. "Even though Somerset is like the end of the earth, the family lived a very cosmopolitan life."

"You mean they ate chocolate, vanilla, and strawberry ice cream?" Michael said.

Everyone stared at him. Suddenly Wanda laughed. "That's *neopolitan,*" she said.

"I mean they kept up with the outside world," Mizriz Sawyer explained. "They would entertain real fancy, especially at Christmas and weddings. The house would sparkle with sperm candles. They would feast on oysters and champagne. It was a regular *Tuskarora frolik!*"

"Yuck!" the children said together. Michael's neopolitan ice cream sounded better, Wendy thought.

Mizriz Sawyer ignored them. "The Collinses had brought pianos from New York and so there was always lots of music. They played charades and had quadrilles."

"I know what charades are," Wendy said, cupping her hand around her ear the way you did in the *sounds like* part of the game, "but what are quadrilles?"

"Dances," Mizriz Sawyer answered. "One time, Mr. Collins even got the crazy idea that everyone at Somerset would talk only in French." She chuckled to herself. "But no one could speak or understand it except him! He thought his blood was the bluest, his opinions the wisest, and his tastes the truests."

"He had blue blood?" Michael asked.

"No," said Wendy, "that's just an expression that means his ancestors were important."

"Everyone's ancestors are important," Wanda said.

Wendy nodded in agreement. "How did Joe 3 wind up with Somerset Place?" she asked.

"In those days they believed in *primogeniture,* which meant the oldest son got the land."

"That doesn't sound too fair," said Marc.

"It wasn't fair," Mizriz Sawyer agreed, staring out the window into the night. "Like slavery — that's why they made them both illegal."

Wendy looked out the window too. "It's so lonesome here," she said.

"That's why the *visit* was the chief form of entertainment for the Collinses," Mizriz Sawyer told them.

"But people visit all the time," Michael said.

"Not then," said Marc. "You didn't just hop in the car and run over to see your best friend."

"That's right," Wanda said. "It would be a big trip to get here from anywhere."

"What did they do when they got here?" Wendy asked.

"Oh wonderful things," Mizriz Sawyer said. "Take walks around the lawn . . . ride horses . . . play the piano — read. Reading was a great pastime at the lake. The Collinses and the Pettigrews both had libraries."

"That would be super to have your own library," Marc said.

That didn't sound too exciting to Wendy.

"And they had fancy weddings," Wanda added. "With a big cake. Just like Mr. Snoad and Miss Allison will have next week."

Now that sounds better, Wendy thought.

"Were the Pettigrews and Collinses good friends?" Wendy asked.

Mizriz Sawyer began stirring again slowly. "Ebenizer Pettigrew had the *spirit of conviction,*" she said.

"She means he was super religious," Wanda whispered.

"After his wife died, he retreated from the world. He said he was just a poor man. A farmer of the swamp not fit for society. *Zuzus!*" she cried suddenly. "I'm supposed to be making cookies, not chit-chat," she exclaimed, grinding her spoon through the batter.

"I can't wait till they're done," Wanda said.

"Me, either," agreed Michael, sneaking his own finger into the bowl for a sample of the thick, sweet goo. Giggling, Wanda aimed her finger into the bowl.

Wendy figured Mizriz Sawyer was like her teacher and didn't miss a trick. "All right you two," she scolded, swatting them both on the seat with the back of a fat, wooden spoon.

"You wash!" she barked at Wendy, pointing to the sink.

Marc smiled. That's not fair, Wendy thought. Just because she was a girl didn't mean she should be the one to wash the dishes.

Marc seemed to read her mind. "I do all the dishes at home," he said. Wendy blushed. She sunk her hands down into the hot water. Standing on her toes, she leaned over the wide sink full of suds and pressed her face against the window. Just as she did, a hairy face popped up out of nowhere, their noses pressed together against the pane of glass.

5 Easter Morning Mystery

Wendy shrieked and fell, elbow-deep, into the suds.

"Good evening!" the bearded, red face called cheerfully. The cheeks were puffy. The voice was high and shrill like a bird's. The fat face disappeared.

"That beast of a man scared me to death," Wendy said. "Who is he?"

Mizriz Sawyer pursed her lips and squinted her eyes. "He thinks he's *Lord Consequence.*"

"Truth or Consequence?" Michael asked.

Marc grabbed a dish towel and tucked it in the neck of his tee shirt like a bib and bowed deeply. He pranced up and down the kitchen waving his spoon. "Mr. Pumpelly is Somerset's restoration expert," he said, in the man's chirpy voice. "He goes around peeling paint and wallpaper to see what used to be under there. Then, he writes reports in fancy cursive on how to make the house look be-u-ti-ful."

They all giggled at Marc's imitation.

"How do they know what things looked like to restore them?" Wendy asked.

Marc snatched the towel from his shirt. "They do research," he said. "Lots of reading."

"And they ask people," Wanda added.

"Like who?" asked Michael.

"People who might have lived and worked around here in the past," Marc said.

"Like my mama," Mizriz Sawyer said proudly.

"That's right," Wanda said. "They came to talk to my grandma one time. She told them a lot about Somerset. They tape recorded everything she said. Mr. Pumpelly plays the tapes over and over."

"But . . ." Mizriz Sawyer bellowed. "He thinks they should raise the water in the lake . . . wants to put in a rice garden like they used to have — flood practically up to the house. Next he'll be wanting slaves to farm it," she grumbled.

Wendy could understand how Mizriz Sawyer wouldn't think that going back to slave days would be too great. She couldn't even imagine being a slave, even though she felt like one sometimes when Grandmother ordered her around cleaning house on Saturdays. But it sure must not be any fun to be a slave all your life and know your children would be slaves too, she thought.

"They ought to leave the lake just like it is," the woman shrilled. "It's not smart to mess with nature . . . nature knows what she wants. You start messin' with mother nature and she'll mess with you."

"But they need to regulate the water level," Marc argued. "Dad says Lake Phelps is an example of ecological succession," Marc said.

Wendy looked at him, wondering if he were making that up. "Yeah?" she said.

Instead of his usual smug look, Marc explained eagerly, "I mean the changing water level of the lake. It's high for a few years and you have a cypress swamp. Then the water level drops."

"Is that why the water used to be so close to the house when I was little?" asked Wanda.

"Yes," Marc said. "But now with the lake used by so many people for different reasons, we need to manage the water level. Help nature out — not hurt it."

That sounded reasonable to Wendy, especially if it meant she would get to move here.

Mizriz Sawyer looked aggravated. "You chirrun get out of here," she said. "Let me get these cookies baking, or we won't have any zuzus for Easter."

Easter morning dawned with a beautiful sunrise. The sky looked like a rainbow of raspberry and orange and pineapple sherbet. Shiny dew was sprinkled over everything.

A muffled noise in The Village woke Wendy up before everyone else. She put her sneakers on under her gown and jogged to the lake. When she reached the end of the mansion where the bridge over the canal and the path to the Pettigrew place were, she stopped to rest.

It was as quiet as a graveyard — when all the ghosts were sleeping. Or at least she hoped they were. She straddled the root of a big cypress tree and leaned back against the enormous trunk. She stared out at the glistening, blue water. She could just imagine living on the other side of the lake. They would have a pier with a little boat so she and Uncle Ed could row over to Somerset Place. She could jog and ride Charley Horse all she wanted to.

Behind her, Wendy heard the soft pump of footsteps on the grass. She was afraid to turn around. What if it were the beast?

The footsteps came closer, then stopped. She knew that whatever it was, it was on the other side of the tree. She could even hear it breathing.

Whipping around, all she could see was the wide trunk of the tree.

Suddenly, it came out from behind the tree. It was Marc.

"Good morning — Happy Easter," he said cheerfully. She could tell by the deep dent of the dimples in his cheeks that he had scared her on purpose.

She refused to let him know that he had succeeded. "Happy Easter," she said and gritted her teeth into a smile.

Wanda and Michael came running up. "Your Uncle Ed says we can hunt for the eggs!" Wanda squealed.

"Yes!" said Michael. "He says they're hidden all over the yard. The one who finds the most gets a prize!"

Wendy looked up and frowned. The early bird was supposed to get the worm. Here she had been the first one up and she hadn't seen a single egg. The hollowed bottoms of the cypress trees made a perfect place to hide eggs. So did the clumps of tall, green grass.

By now, Uncle Ed, Mizriz Sawyer, and Mr. Walker had come outside and were watching the children scurry around the yard like bunny rabbits, searching for eggs.

"Aw, c'mon," Uncle Ed teased, "I didn't hide them that hard."

"You didn't hide them easy either," Michael complained, poking his head deep in the side of a cypress tree. He reappeared empty handed.

"I hard-boiled a million of them," Mizriz Sawyer cried across the yard. "Yellow and pink and blue."

"I'd be glad to just find one," Wanda said.

They searched the edges of the yard. Then they retraced their paths, checking places they had already scoured once.

Uncle Ed looked puzzled. He stuck his head into the tree where Michael had looked and pulled it back out. "Now I know I hid an egg at the base of this tree," he said. "And I put one over there in the bushes where Wanda was just looking."

"I know you hid them, too," Wendy said. "I heard you this morning when I first got up."

"You did?" Uncle Ed said with great surprise.

"Didn't I?" asked Wendy, teasingly, knowing Uncle Ed wouldn't like to be caught hiding the eggs. She smiled at him, then the corner of her mouth fell into a frown. "I didn't, did I?" she asked.

He shook his head. "I hid the eggs last night before I went to bed!"

"So whoever I heard this morning wasn't *hiding* eggs — they were *hunting* them," Wendy said in dismay.

"And they found them," said Marc.

"Stole them!" said Wanda, tossing her basket on the ground.

"Yeah," Michael said disappointedly. He plopped on the grass with his chin on his knees.

Wendy felt sorry for him. He was the youngest and she knew an egg hunt was a big treat for him. And now someone had stolen all the eggs. But why?

Uncle Ed looked angry. "Whoever did this, it's a stupid trick," he said.

"I wonder if it's our water level report thief?" said Mr. Walker.

But Wendy wondered if beasts liked eggs.

Suddenly the sun peeked over the edge of the lake and glistened across the water like a silver spear. A group of cars pulled into the parking area. Waving and smiling, the visitors walked up the drive toward the mansion. The grim group just stood there and stared back at them.

"Sunrise service time," Mizriz Sawyer called, hurrying across the yard to greet the guests. Uncle Ed and Mr. Walker followed, talking in low, hushed voices. Wanda and Michael took one last hopeful look around the yard.

"What did you see this morning?" Marc asked eagerly.

Wendy hesitated. He had not believed her before. She did not really want to be ridiculed anymore by some stubborn boy. But he was pretty smart, she thought, and she needed all the help she could get. "I heard a man moving around the yard," she said, "in and out of the trees, stopping every now and then."

"*Un*-hiding eggs," Marc said. "Are you sure it was a man?"

Wendy frowned at him. She should have known he wouldn't believe her.

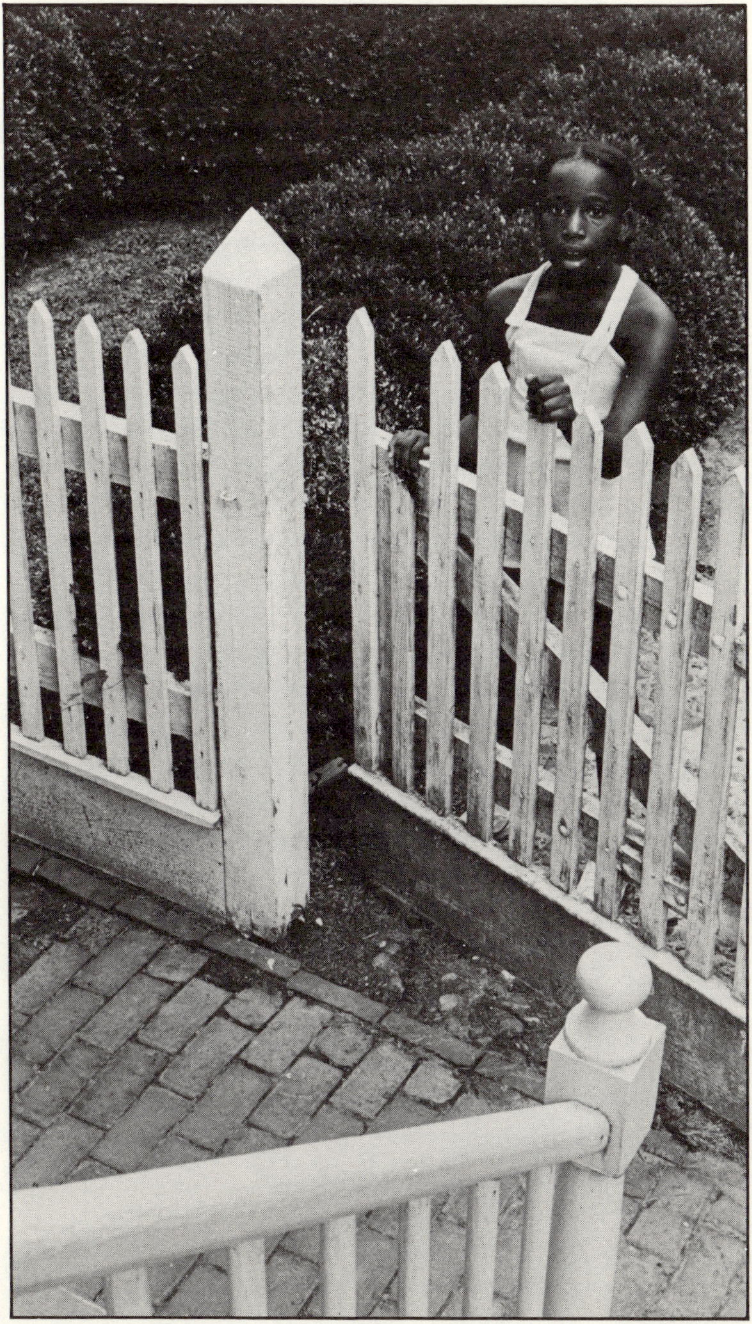

"I just mean a woman could be a thief too, you know," he said stubbornly.

"That's true," she agreed. "I didn't look out the window so I don't really know."

Uncle Ed hollered for them to hurry up.

As Wendy started running to The Gate House to change clothes, Marc grabbed her arm. "Do you think . . ." he began, ". . . do you think it was the beast?"

6 A Slippery, Wet Clue

Wendy stopped and shrugged her shoulders. "I just don't know," she admitted, glad that at least he finally believed her.

By the time Wendy dressed and ran back to the mansion, the minister was standing at the edge of the canal. There were rows of folding chairs on the porch where the adults sat. But Wendy perched on a corner where the banisters met. She wrapped an arm around the post to keep her balance.

Now this is the kind of church I like, she thought. Out in the cool, open air with the birds chirping. She wiggled her toes. Where you can wear shorts and go barefoot.

Wendy went to church with her grandmother each Sunday in Atlanta. But it was a big downtown church — so big that the minister had to use two loud microphones. You had to dress up and sit still and be quiet. The TV cameras would stare at the congregation during the hymns, which made her nervous.

She figured God probably didn't really care where you had church. What did her grandmother always quote? *Wherever two or three gather in my name, there I am also.*

She couldn't help but wonder if the beast were here too this morning. She looked up and down the rows of people on the porch. All the Somerset people were here. Michael's mom had brought his sister, Michele. John and Jo Dee and Brian had come over from Bath. And there were a lot of local Creswell and Columbia people she didn't know.

Were any of them the beast? She caught Marc's eyes wandering and wondered if he were thinking about the same thing.

They were singing the closing hymn and Wendy realized she hadn't heard one word of the sermon. Just like real church, she thought, and turned toward the lake so no one would see her giggle. She winced at the brilliant sunlight on the lake. The water was rippled just like the old panes of glass in the house. Between the bright bumps of water, she thought she could see a small boat heading toward the opposite shore.

She said a short prayer to help her find the report so her uncle could buy his land. She also had an ugly thought about the beast and figured that wasn't too great a thing to think at church, so added quickly, *bless the beast.* Bless the beast?! Wendy giggled out loud now.

As soon as the minister said *Amen,* the other kids came running over to her. "What's so funny?" they asked. She slid off her perch. "Nothing," she fibbed, giggling again.

"That's for sure," said Michael, still disappointed over the missing eggs.

Everyone headed for the white cloths spread out over the green lawn. Michele and Brian and Jo Dee were already sprawled on one blanket. They each had heaping plates of scrambled eggs, grits, hot homemade biscuits — and zuzus, of course. Wendy and Wanda edged in on one side of the cloth to join the group. Marc and Michael sprawled on the grass next to them.

Wendy took one big, chewy bite of zuzus, then got down to business. "Tell us how you solved the missing head mystery over in Bath last summer?" she asked Michele.

The kids from Bath stared at her in surprise, their food paused halfway between their mouths and their plates.

"Why?" asked Michele. "Have you got a mystery at Somerset Place?"

"We sure do!" Wendy said. She told all that had happened to them so far. Marc and Michael and Wanda burst in after every other word to add to the mysterious story.

Wendy did like to read mystery books. She was especially fond of the *History Mystery* series by Carole Marsh. *The Missing Head Mystery* that Michele and Michael and Brian and Jo Dee were in was super. She had learned a lot about North Carolina history when she read it.

But she sure wished that Ms. Marsh had written a book about Somerset Place so that she would know better where to look for clues. Oh well, maybe if she solved the mystery, Ms. Marsh would write a book about her and the haunt of beasts. But that was just daydreaming, she thought. She had better get back to reality or she'd still be living in Atlanta instead of on Lake Phelps.

"A beast!" said Michele, in admiration of their problem.

"That's about as bad as a headless pirate," Brian said.

"Worse!" claimed Wanda.

"Especially if you've seen it," Wendy added.

"I can sure see why you need to solve this mystery so bad and so fast," Michele said.

Brian shook his head and frowned. "You need one thing that you don't have."

"What?" Wendy begged.

"Clues," he said.

"We thought we'd never get any clues," Michele said. "Then we were flooded with them."

"Red herrings, most of them," Jo Dee added.

"Herrings!" Marc shouted and jumped up. "The herring are running today." He tore across the yard. "C'mon!" he shouted back to them.

"What's he talking about?" Wendy asked.

"The herring," said Wanda. "They open the watergates in the canal and the fish rush in and you can catch them with nets."

With one big gulp of cocoa Wendy ran after Marc and the others.

Everyone was lined up on either side of the canal in front of the mansion. Water gushed through the canal like the log flume ride at Disney World. Wendy leaned over the edge and peered into the foam. She could see the herring swimming fiercely like she did her free-

A Slippery, Wet Clue

style stroke. Some people had nets. They dipped them in the canal, then dumped the dripping, squiggling fish into baskets.

Marc thrust a small net at her. Grabbing it, Wendy dug into the water.

"This is fun," Michael said. He was dumping more fish on the ground than he was in his basket. Wanda dipped her fish out slowly and neatly.

Before long, Wendy was sopping wet from her neck to her knees. Even the ends of her straight, brown hair were as shiny and wet as the fish.

"Look!" Michael squealed suddenly. His voice was urgent above the laughing and talking and splashing.

Wendy glanced across the canal at him. "What is it?" she hollered back, expecting him to show her another fish.

He shoved his net across the canal at her, almost pushing his fish into her face.

By now, Michael's frantic commotion had Marc and Wanda's attention too. "Yeah, what is it?" Marc said, leaning over Wendy's shoulder to look into the basket.

When she reached to take the net from Michael, Wendy slipped and splashed head first into the canal. She jumped straight up, fish scurrying past her, tickling her legs. Everyone rushed over to help her out. But she just stood in the water ignoring everyone and staring down into Michael's net which she still gripped tightly.

"It's a clue," she said. *"It's a clue!"*

7 The Lost Lake

Uncle Ed pulled Wendy, dripping like a wet herring, from the water. "I caught the biggest fish," he teased. Everyone laughed, glad that she had not been hurt.

Phooey, Wendy thought, her face turning red. *If they knew what a good swimmer I am, they wouldn't worry about me falling in a crummy, old canal.*

"I'd better get some dry clothes on," she said, pulling free from her uncle. Mostly, she was just eager to get away and show the others what had been found.

She rushed toward The Gate House. The others followed behind her, Michael dragging his basket of fish. Wendy took the shortcut through the English garden by the mansion. As soon as they disappeared in the maze of bushes where no one could see them, she stopped.

"What is it?" Wanda begged, trying to peek into the net.

"You won't believe it!" Michael said.

Marc just stooped down beside Wendy and demanded, "Show us!"

Thrusting her hand down under the wet, slippery fish, Wendy pulled out a mysterious pink object and held it up.

"An egg!" Michael said. "One of the missing Easter eggs."

"A *clue*," Wendy corrected him, turning the egg to show them the writing on one side. "Michael was the one who really found it," she added.

"You're a good egg, Michael," Marc teased, patting him on the back. "Let's just hope it's not a red herring."

"What's that?" Michael asked.

"You might say it's a fishy clue," Marc replied.

Michael looked puzzled.

"He means it's a false clue that leads you on a wild goose chase," Wendy explained.

"Won't you please just read the egg," Wanda pleaded.

"It looks like it's been written with marker, so it's a little blurred from the water," Wendy said. "But I think it says:

'Something lost you're looking for?
You do not need to look too far.
First look high and then look low,
Finder's Island is the place to go.'"

Wendy shook her straggly, wet hair. "Finder's Island?" she said.

"Is that an island out in the middle of the lake?"

Michael asked.

"There aren't any islands in the lake," Wanda answered.

Wendy looked at Marc. He read so much that she knew he would know. Boy, to think she had to depend on an eggheaded boy to solve this mystery! He looked back at her with a smug grin.

"I-know-that-you-know-that-I-know-that-you-know," she said.

Marc laughed. "Finder's Island isn't in the lake," he explained.

"Then how can it be an island?" Wendy complained. "Islands are bodies of land completely surrounded by water," she quoted from her geography book.

"Well, this one isn't," Marc retorted. "It's a mound of land near the lake. When some hunters were first trying to find the lake, one of them climbed a tree and got up high enough to see it. But Joe 3 ran and got into the water first, so he claimed the right to name it Lake Phelps."

"So that's why they call it Finder's Island," Wendy said. She jumped up, tipping the basket of herring over in the grass.

"I wish I could discover a lake," said Michael.

"I wish I could find that report!" Wendy said. "Let's go to Finder's Island and look. Maybe it's in the base of a cypress tree or something."

Marc just squatted on the ground. "I don't know where it is," he confessed. "The way the lake water rises and falls — sometimes the mound is underwater, and sometimes it isn't. Besides, there are a lot of mounds of land around that side of the lake."

Oh, brother, Wendy thought. She was afraid this wasn't going to be easy. "Well, we'll just have to look at all of them," she said. "And the sooner, the better. What if the thief hid the report there and then the lake rises and floats it away?"

"That's possible," Marc agreed. "But the lake level's down now, because they've let the water into the canals for the herring run."

"Then this really would be a good time to look, wouldn't it?" Wanda said.

"What if the beast is out there?" Michael asked.

"Oh, bless the beast," Wendy said, and the others giggled. But silently she thought she didn't really want to find a beast on Finder's Island.

"Wendy! Michael!" a voice called.

"We've been found," Michael said.

A head popped between two bushes. "Thought you had gone home to get dry," Uncle Ed scolded. "Hurry it up! We're going to ride over to Columbia for a while."

Wendy and the others groaned.

During the drive to Columbia, they talked about Somerset Place.

"Well," said Mr. Walker, "In 100 years the lifestyle here improved from hunters in the wilderness to wealthy planters with slaves."

"Some improvement," Wanda grumbled.

"But look what happened to the rich farmers," Marc said. "They finally lost everything."

"That's right," Mr. Walker agreed. "Their way of life has disappeared. The families of the hunters went on to survive the isolation, the weather, and the disease here — and the end of the slavery."

Wendy was confused. "How did it work out that way?"

"Probably because they were never dependent on slaves for their livelihood," Mr. Walker said.

Wendy saw a funny look come over Wanda's face, as though she didn't understand all that Marc's dad had said, but she looked secretly happy that the Collinses' way of life had disappeared.

"From the construction of the Collins Canal to the end of the Civil War, the plantation operated only because of the slaves," Uncle Ed said.

"Mama told me Mr. Pettigrew once said he wished there weren't a slave in the world," said Wanda.

"Mr. Collins tried to be good to his slaves," Mr. Walker said. "But it was difficult to always be fair about working the slaves when everything they did was so necessary for life here."

"Why didn't the slaves just leave?" Wendy asked, thinking she sure wouldn't stick around.

"Where would they have gone?" asked Uncle Ed. "Somerset was their home too."

"Slavery seems long ago and far away," Wendy said. "Like something we read about in history at school."

"Well, it might be to you," Mr. Walker said. "But there are a lot of families still around this area whose parents and grandparents worked at Somerset."

"As slaves?" Michael asked.

"Of course," said Wanda. "Just like my grandma."

"Your grandmother was a slave?" Michael asked.

"Of course," Wanda said.

"Boy, I'd like to meet her," Michael said, as

though she were a celebrity.

"Is your mama a slave too?" he asked.

"No!" said Wanda. "She works at Somerset because she likes it — not because somebody bought her like a . . . like a car or something."

By the time they returned to Somerset Place, it was almost night.

The Village was dark. From somewhere, Captain Horniblow, the owl, gave a spooky *whooot*. The mansion and buildings looked abandoned. A gray mist sifted down through the branches of the cypress trees. It was like a Hollywood set for a scary movie, Wendy thought. It truly looked like a *haunt of beasts*.

The adults all stopped at The Gate House to have coffee. Wendy and the others huddled on the front porch steps. After a lot of hurried whispering, they sent Wanda inside.

"Can we please go to The Big House and get some zuzus?" they heard her ask politely.

"Help yourself!" Mizriz Sawyer boomed.

Wanda stormed through the screen door. She flashed them her biggest, brightest smile.

"Let's go!" Wendy said, and they began running to find the mysterious island in the clue.

About halfway to the lake, Marc stopped dead still. Wendy plowed into the back of him. Wanda stumbled into her, and Michael into Wanda. They all argued at each other at once.

"Hush," said Marc. "Look!"

"I don't believe it," Wendy said in a whisper as soft as the gray dusk.

"Me, either," said Wanda, peering around her.

Michael just stared.

Then all together, they said what they were seeing, or rather what they were *not* seeing.

"The lake is gone!"

8 A Scare on Finder's Island

"The lake is gone," Wendy repeated in disbelief. You could always see it from here, the water lapping at the tall swamp grass.

Marc had run on ahead of them. He was standing on a pile of old bricks with his hands on his hips when Wendy caught up.

"Well, it really isn't gone," he said, "but look at how low the water level is. Somebody's been messing with it."

"I wonder *who?*" Wendy said.

"We know," Marc said.

"Yeah, except that we don't know," Wendy replied. "That's the problem."

Wanda and Michael had run back to get Uncle Ed. The adults hurried toward the lake, with the two kids leading the way.

Uncle Ed stomped past Wendy and Marc and strode out across the puddle of a lake. "Well, I'll be . . ."

Wendy figured he would have added a bad word at the end if they hadn't been there. She could sure say a few blankety blanks herself.

Mr. Walker had run over to the canal and was coming back. "Someone opened the watergate after we closed it," he said.

"They're gonna kill our lake," Mizriz Sawyer wailed. She plodded toward the mansion, flapping her apron and mumbling loudly to herself about nature. Wendy thought she heard her say the word *beast.*

Uncle Ed stalked off to call the sheriff and Mr. Walker went to get his measuring instruments.

"Well," said Marc. "Now would be as good a time as any to find Finder's Island."

He began to walk around the edge of the lake through the thick, gooey mud the receding water had left behind. The others followed single-file, like a band of Tuscarora Indians might have done long ago when the lake was free to rise and fall without any interference from people.

As they plodded away from the mansion, the swamp seemed to gobble them up. The thick black bog sucked their feet down with every step.

"Yuck!" said Michael. "Look at my shoes."

As they got farther away from the house, Wendy noticed that Michael moved closer toward the others and watched for any sign of the beast. Wanda and Wendy climbed a little higher on the bank where the mud was not as thick. Marc began to weave in and out of the trees.

Wendy could see a hump of land ahead, and headed straight for it. She climbed the small hill. "I think I've found it!" she shouted.

They all came running as fast as the bog and undergrowth would let them.

Wanda, Michael and Wendy began to search frantically for the report.

Marc just stood at the bottom of the hill shaking his head.

"Aren't you even going to help look?" Wendy complained.

Marc slung his arms up in the air and let them drop to his side. "This isn't Finder's Island," he said.

"But you said it was a mound of dirt beside the lake with trees on it," Wendy recalled.

"I did — and it is," Marc agreed. "But look on ahead," he said with a sweep of his arm.

Looking up from her view on the hill, Wendy groaned. Dozens of mounds of dirt with trees stretched before her. "Oh, brother," she said. "How will we ever know which one is Finder's Island?"

"I guess we won't till we find it," Wanda said.

"That might take forever," Michael figured.

"We don't have forever!" Wendy smiled. "Besides," she added, "what makes you so sure that we haven't gotten lucky for a change. Maybe this *is* Finder's Island?"

Marc stood stubbornly at the bottom of the hill. He shook his head again. "Some of the islands have names," he said. "See that tree? It's a chestnut oak. An old one that probably was here when the lake was discovered. One of the islands was called Chestnut Oak Island, and I think this might be it. But you can look anyway," he added.

Wendy plunked down on a log. "No," she said with

a sigh. She figured he was probably right. "I guess we'll just have to split up and search each island."

"But what if the beast is out there?" Wanda said.

"We won't be that far apart," Marc said. "You can holler if you see something." He stalked off along the edge of the water.

Wendy could see that he believed he could find the island without any help from them. Wanda and Michael were sprawled out under the chestnut oak. She knew they wouldn't look anymore until they got good and ready.

Wendy gazed forlornly around at what now seemed like a bumpy sea of islands. Oh well, she thought, skidding down the side of the hill back into the muck — you have to start somewhere.

Since Marc was determined to explore the lake edge, she decided she would head inland a little way. Because the lake was higher than the land around it, she soon could not see the lake or the other kids.

A low, hooting sound wafted through the woods. Wendy wondered if Captain Horniblow had followed them. Maybe he was trying to tell her something — like *get out of here.*

She searched half a dozen islands with no luck. It had been a long time since that beautiful Easter sunrise and breakfast. She was tired and hungry. The tall cypress trees seemed to gobble up the last light of day. The light left around her faded to purple.

Wendy leaned against the trunk of a tree and yawned. She decided that she had better go back and try again tomorrow.

Suddenly, she heard the sharp crackle of a branch, as though a foot had snapped it. *Just my imagination,* she thought. Then there was a rustle of leaves and another branch popped. She jerked and felt the rough bark of the tree scrape against her back. It's nothing, she thought. The woods are full of noises.

Now behind her, there was the crunch ... crunch...crunch of several footsteps in a row. She mashed her body even closer against the trunk. She felt like she was part of the tree. If she stuck out her arms they would be branches, her fingers would be leaves.

Maybe it's just Marc trying to scare me?

She couldn't stand it any longer. Jerking away from the tree, she spun around. Suddenly, the forest exploded in a symphony of crackling branches and crunching leaves. In the almost black dusk, she saw the raggedy, brown beast running away from her toward the lake.

"Marc!" she screamed, not knowing if she were trying to warn him to run away or beg him to catch the beast.

Losing her balance, she fell forward. There was another crunch. Something gooey crushed beneath her hand. She was afraid to look down.

Squinting her eyes so she couldn't see the mysterious mess too well, she lifted her hand. With relief, she saw that it wasn't a frog. And with joy, she realized what the crushed green mess was.

"Marc!" she screamed again into the forest.

9 The Little Attic Room

There wasn't a sound in the forest. Not of man nor beast, Wendy thought. She giggled at the phrase in spite of herself. Gingerly, she picked up the squashed mess and rushed toward the mansion side of the lake.

Snarled roots grabbed her feet. Tangled limbs snatched her hair. Just when she felt completely lost, the trees parted and she saw The Big House. A flashlight was scanning the edge of the lake and she ran toward it.

"Where have you been?" Uncle Ed fumed. "We've been worried to death. There's enough mysterious messing around going on without you disappearing," he said.

He was mad all right. But Wendy could tell he was glad to see her.

"I don't know if Somerset is the place for you to live," he said earnestly. "I'd have to hunt for you every night."

"Oh no, Uncle Ed," she promised. "No you wouldn't!"

The other kids had been keeping a lookout for her. They hung over the porch of the second floor balcony of the mansion and waved and shouted.

"You get home now and get a bath," Uncle Ed said softly, gently pulling a twig from her tangled hair.

Wendy waved up to them. "Can't I please tell the others good night first," she begged.

Uncle Ed shook his head in dismay. Just like Grandmother always does, Wendy thought. "Hurry it up," he warned.

By the time Wendy reached the front porch of the house, the others had already charged down the stairs and met her at the door.

"Come in here!" Marc ordered, yanking her into the hall.

"Where did you go?" Michael asked.

"We thought you got lost!" Wanda said.

"Yeah, your uncle was really worried," Marc added. Wendy could tell that they had been too.

"I found Finder's Island," she blurted.

"How do you know?" Marc said, doubtfully.

Wendy just smiled and opened her hands. In the dim hall light they all peered down at the jumble of green, yellow and white.

"What's that?" Wanda asked.

Now Marc smiled. He reached into Wendy's palms and turned the object over. "It's an egg," he said.

"A squashed egg," Wendy added and giggled. "I was afraid I'd mashed a frog."

"Schoooo-weee!" Michael squealed, pinching his nose. He bent over and held his stomach at the thought.

"Shhh," Wendy warned. They moved close to the hall table. A soft lamp threw spooky shadows across the ceiling.

"Can you still read it?" Michael whispered.

Marc poked his nose down close to the smelly mess. "The writing's cracked through."

Wendy laid the lump next to the lamp and slowly read:

*" 'Bee tree, moccasin, 30, mountain, western —
All lead to the second forest.'*

"Oh, brother," Wendy said. "If that stupid beast thinks I'm dumb enough to go back out in the forest . . ." she began.

"I should hope not!" Mizriz Sawyer cried from the doorway. "You plumb gave us a fright."

Wendy scooped the egg up and stuffed it in her back jeans pocket.

"You chirrun get in the kitchen and have a snack," Mizriz Sawyer ordered. "Then it's bedtime for all of you."

They followed her through the dark rooms of the mansion and out the side door. After the chill of the forest at night, it was warm and cozy in the kitchen.

Mizriz Sawyer had put a plate of cookies and a big glass of milk for each of them around the table in the center of the room.

Wendy hopped up on a stool. She felt the egg smush even more when she sat down. Thank goodness it's not a frog, she thought. She took a big gulp of milk and a giant bite of cookie. Everyone was gobbling away.

Suddenly her mouth flew open. Milk drizzled down the side of her chin. Cookie crumbs flew as she blurted breathlessly, "Oh, yeah, I almost forgot . . . I saw the beast!"

The next morning it was raining fiercely. Wendy propped herself up in her bed on the second floor of The Gate House and yawned. The house was quiet. The only sound was the splat of raindrops on the roof and the gush of water through the gutters.

Wendy scooted to the edge of the bed and looked out the window. The Village was a wet mass of green. There was no one in sight. The huddle of small dripping buildings looked like they could silently float away. The mist sneaking around the mansion made it look like a haunted house. Wendy shivered.

She dressed quickly. Grabbing Uncle Ed's old black umbrella and yellow rain slicker, she hurried toward The Big House.

Since the ground was like a lake itself today, Wendy stayed on the walkways. The long curved stretches of brick were slippery. A little canal of water flooded down each side.

The mansion was gloomy. Low lights flickered and raindrops slithered down the wavery panes of glass.

Wendy heard giggling, and followed the sound into the library. Marc, Michael, and Wanda were playing cards.

"Mizriz Sawyer taught us to play *whist,*" Michael greeted her.

"And I'm winning," Wanda said proudly.

Marc frowned. "Nothing else to do today except

play cards with a bunch of kids," he grumbled. "It's even too wet for you to look for your clue," he added, almost cheerfully, Wendy thought.

"Oh, no, it's not," she countered. "I *have* to look — rain or shine. Uncle Ed left me a note saying he has gone to talk to Mr. Snoad about the property. I'm afraid he'll tell him he's going to have to back out of the deal if the report isn't found soon."

"Where's the egg?" asked Wanda.

"It was beginning to stink," Wendy said. "I threw it away." She pulled a piece of paper out of her pocket and read the clue she had copied off of the egg: *"Bee tree, moccasin, 30, mountain, western — All lead to the second forest."*

"What's a bee tree?" Michael asked. Wendy could tell that he wasn't interested in looking for that.

"And a moccasin?" Wanda said. "A snake or a shoe?"

Marc folded his cards and stretched his chair back on two legs. "They're canals," he said. "Those are the names of canals."

"You mean there's more than the one in front of the mansion?" Wendy marveled.

"Oh, sure," Marc said. "There are a lot of canals that run from the lake through the fields."

"But what's the *second forest?*" Michael interrupted.

Wendy glanced quickly at Marc hoping he had the answer — even if he would act proud to know-it-all.

Marc let his chair bang back against the floor. "I don't know," he said.

"I hope it's not over at the Pettigrew Place," Wendy said. "I just wish we could figure out who the thief is. Maybe it's someone who used to live at Somerset Place?" she suggested.

"There are a lot of old mysteries and legends about this area," Marc said.

"Like what?" Wendy asked. She bet he was going to make up a lot of stupid stories to try and scare them.

"I know one," said Wanda. "The little Collins boys drowned in the canal. They were playing on a raft with two of the slave children. Somehow they fell off and drowned."

"Couldn't they swim?" asked Michael. Wendy knew he had won ribbons in his swim team meets last summer.

"Mama said the water was icy cold. A man tried to save them. But he was so shocked by the cold water that someone had to rescue him."

"That's terrible," Wendy said, remembering how fiercely the water had rushed around her when she fell in the canal. "But the thief is sure not the ghost of two little boys," she added.

"Then how about this?" Marc said, going to the front window. "Another Collins was riding his horse on the carriage drive. He was thrown against a tree and killed."

They all stared down the rows of gloomy, dripping sycamore trees swaying in the wind.

"Joe 3 had a heavy chain fastened around the tree which strangled it to death," Marc went on.

"He could want to come back and haunt his old home," Michael agreed.

"And then," Marc said spookily, "there are two mysteries about the attic."

"That's right!" Wanda said, as if she had just remembered something she would rather forget.

"Tell us," Michael begged bravely.

"I'll *show* you," Marc said, marching off.

They followed him up the narrow, curved staircase to the second floor. There was a big, open hall with bedrooms and balconies leading off of it. Marc motioned to a small, skinny flight of stairs.

"They say that the Collinses had a retarded daughter," said Wanda. "They were supposed to have kept her hid in the attic and fed her through a secret panel."

"That's dumb," Wendy said. "Retarded people are people too. We even had a special class for them at my school in Atlanta. They're not something to be ashamed of. They have feelings."

"We know that," said Marc, "but in the Collins' day, people didn't know better and they did stupid things like that."

"Yes," added Wanda soberly. "Like blacks — they thought we were different too. We weren't free either — or believed to have any feelings," she said, looking up the staircase.

Marc led the way and opened the door. Wendy had to blink her eyes several times before she could see in the dim light.

She thought it was the neatest place she had ever seen. There was a big room where they kept trunks. And another big room had been the nursery.

The strange, curved ceiling came to a point over a small door.

"What's that room?" Michael asked.

"The cooling room," Marc said.

"Ok, we give up," Wendy said. "What's a cooling room?"

"When anyone died, they put the body in there to stay until they could have a funeral and bury it," Wanda told them.

"Yuck!" Michael said.

Wanda and Michael explored the children's nursery. Marc crawled around the baseboards feeling for a secret panel.

Stooping down, Wendy went through the short tunnel to the door of the cooling room. Even though it had glass windows, she couldn't see inside because it was too dark. But she could see that the room had another door with windows. Through that she could see a small garret room.

She wondered if Marc knew anything about that room. She started to ask him, then decided to discover it for herself.

Turning the knob of the cooling room door, she stepped down. Gritting her teeth, she took the few steps through the darkness to reach the other side. She felt like she should say *excuse me* in case she were bumping into any ghosts.

Through the window of the second door, she could see a small table and the end of a bed. There was a big, curved window almost as wide as the room.

Opening the door, she slipped inside to see the view of the lake from this high up. Turning to close the door behind her, she saw the rest of the bed — and what she saw stretched out on it made her jump with fear.

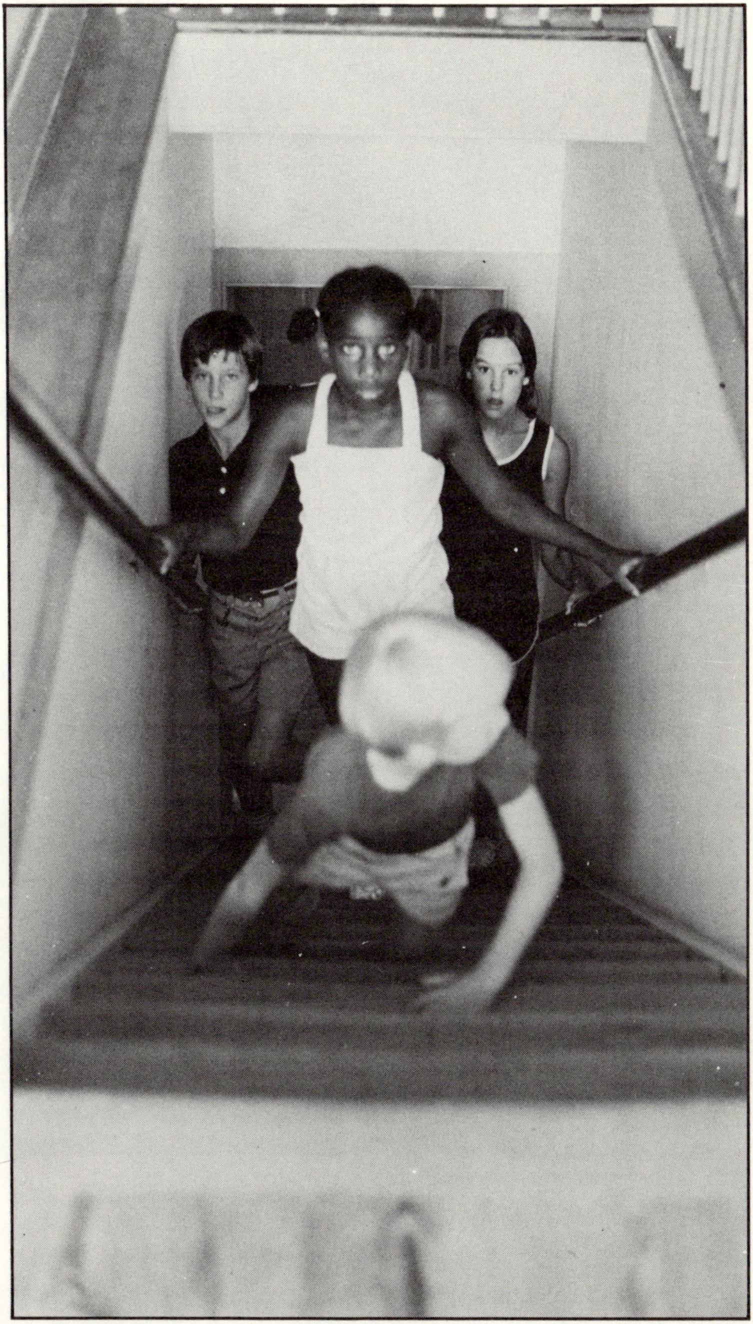

10 Did They Drown?

The man lying on the bed slowly sat up. He rubbed his puffy eyelids.

"Mr. Pumpelly!" Wendy squealed. "You scared me!"

"Huh . . . what? . . ." the man mumbled. He yawned and drug his watch from his vest pocket.

Marc burst into the room. He looked startled to see another person with Wendy. "What's *he* doing here?" he demanded.

"I must have fallen asleep," Mr. Pumpelly said, rolling his sausage legs over the edge of the bed and standing up. He rubbed his red eyes again and put his glasses on.

He peered out over the wire rims at the children and gathered up his things on the table. He inched open a black case like a doctor's bag and stuffed a little knife inside.

By now the man was more awake. He cleared his

throat. "What are *you* doing up here," he demanded. "*I* have business up here."

"We were . . ." Wendy began, then stopped. She didn't want to tell him that they were researching the ghosts of Somerset Place. He'd either only laugh at her or want to know why. And she had a sudden funny feeling that she didn't want him to know.

Whistling and puffing loudly through his nose, Mr. Pumpelly paraded out of the room.

Wendy followed. She just had to giggle when she saw the look on Wanda and Michael's faces when they saw him come out of the cooling room.

"What's Mr. Pumpbelly doing in there?" asked Michael.

Marc came out of the cooling room and closed the door. "That's a good question," he said. "He left this behind."

Wendy looked and shrugged her shoulders. "A pen . . . so what?"

Wanda took the pen from Marc. "It's one of Mama's laundry markers," she said.

"That's right," Marc said, looking at Wendy. "An indelible marker."

"Does that mean you can eat it?" asked Michael.

"Not edible, *indelible,*" Marc repeated.

Suddenly Wendy understood. "The clues on the egg were written in indelible ink. That's why the writing didn't wash off in the canal."

"Exactly," said Marc. "If he had eggs in that little, black case he could have slipped off up here to make some more clues," he added.

"Yes," agreed Wendy. "We know he doesn't want the lake level changed. He could have hidden the re-

Did They Drown?

port right here in the mansion and be using the clues to keep us away."

"Well, if that's what he was doing, I wish we'd caught him in the act," Marc said. "There's no escape from that room."

"That's for sure," said Wendy, turning and looking back through the unusual, curved window. It was quiet in the attic. "Listen," she said. "It's stopped raining. Let's go look for the second forest. I've had enough of this spooky place."

They scooted down two flights of steps and headed toward the front door.

"Stop!" a voice yelled behind them. They groaned and turned around.

"I've been looking all over for you chirrun," Mizriz Sawyer said. She squinted her eyes at Wanda. "You have chores," she said. "Marc, your father wants you to go to Edenton with him." She pointed a finger at Wendy. "And your uncle says you've got reading to do." She turned and waddled back through the house, swatting at everything in sight with her feather duster.

They clumped down the stairs behind her.

Mr. Pumpelly was in the parlor. He gasped and held out his hand when he saw Mizriz Sawyer aim the duster at a priceless vase. She just swatted it, and then his hand, and kept on walking.

"Brother," Wendy said. "We'll never get to check out that clue."

"Let's all get our errands done as fast as we can," Marc suggested. "As each of us finishes, we can take one of the canals and search it."

"Good idea," Wendy agreed, pulling the wrinkled note from her pocket. "Marc, you take Mountain and

I'll take Moccasin. Wanda, you can search 30 canal. And Michael, you take Bee Tree."

Michael frowned. "As long as it doesn't really have any bee trees on it," he said.

By the time Wendy had finished her reading, it was late afternoon. Uncle Ed was delighted that she wanted to read from his historical collection. If he only knew why! It had taken her some extra time to find what she was looking for, but she felt certain it had solved the mystery of the second forest. The only problem was that now she couldn't find any of the others to tell them about it.

The Village was still gloomy and gray. The big cypress trees dripped so much water that it felt like it was still raining when you walked beneath them. And it had turned chilly.

Wendy found Moccasin Canal and strolled alongside it. It was flooded from the rain and looked like a long, skinny lake jutting through the field. Water sloshed angrily back and forth. Sometimes a wave jumped over the narrow sides and splashed her.

Walking steadily toward the lake, Wendy stepped high to avoid the frogs in the tall grass. Soon she could see 30 canal. Running frantically up and down beside it was Marc. He jumped over the canal, then sprinted up and down the other side.

Wendy wondered why he was searching Wanda's canal instead of his own. She walked toward him and waved, but he ignored her. When she got closer, she could see the panic on his face.

"Have you seen Wanda or Michael?" he asked urgently.

"No . . . did you find something?" she asked eagerly.

"Yes," he said, "but not what you think." He shoved a dripping object at her. "It's Wanda's umbrella," he said. "When Dad and I left for Edenton, I saw Michael and her walking around together under it. So when I got back I thought I'd check their canals and see if they had any luck."

"You don't mean . . ." Wendy interrupted, grabbing the soggy umbrella from him.

"I found it floating in the canal," he said in dismay.

Wendy just stood there, letting the water drip off the top of the umbrella into her tennis shoes. She looked up and down the canal. All she could think of were the two little Collins kids. They had drowned in the canals.

"Michael can swim," she said weakly.

"But look at this water," Marc slammed his fist in the air at the rushing canal. "And I don't think Wanda can swim at all," he added.

Wendy felt like the cold water was rushing through her veins. She shivered. It was getting colder.

"You search from here to the road," Marc ordered. "I'll look from here to the lake."

Wendy didn't even think about the bossiness in his voice. This was an emergency. She ran along the canal toward the road, keeping her eyes on the mean, gray water. She felt wet drops on her face, but didn't know if they were rain or tears.

If anything had happened to Wanda and Michael it would be her fault, she thought. She was the one who wanted them to look for another clue. And she was the one who had told them to go ahead and look on their own instead of waiting for her or Marc.

When she reached the road, Wendy had still not seen any sign of them. She turned and took a deep breath and dashed back to see if Marc had discovered anything. She didn't know whether she would feel worse if they found them, or if they didn't. She tried to remember the first aid for drowning she had learned at school.

When she and Marc met, they were both panting so hard they could barely talk.

He motioned toward the trees at the edge of the water. "We need to look around the lake," he said breathlessly.

Wendy shuddered. He was right. The canal led to the lake. And if Michael and Wanda had drowned, then that's where they would have been washed.

They stomped through the wet marsh. Suddenly Wendy gasped. Lying side by side, face down in the swamp by a cypress tree were Wanda and Michael. Before they could reach them, Michael's head popped up. He turned toward them, the front of his clothes dripping with mud. He raised a balled fist in the air. "I found it!" he shouted.

Wendy didn't know whether to laugh or cry. Marc just stood there with his mouth open.

Wanda looked up at them. "We found the next clue," she said proudly, smiling through a mud-caked face.

Wendy just stared at her as though she were a ghost.

"We found *you*," Marc finally said in relief.

Michael glared at him. "We found a clue," he repeated. He shoved the orange egg up into Wendy's face. "Doesn't anybody care?"

"But the umbrella . . ." Wendy began.

"Oh, we dropped it in the canal trying to chase the egg," Wanda explained.

"Then the egg disappeared," Michael said.

"But we ran ahead and found it floating into this cypress tree," Wanda continued.

Wendy sat down in the mud and sighed. "We thought you two had drowned," she confessed.

Michael and Wanda looked at each other in surprise.

"Why would we go and do a thing like that?" Michael asked.

"Well, people don't usually drown on purpose," Marc said, then started laughing uncontrollably. Wendy knew he was just as relieved as she was to find them safe.

"Don't you even want to read the clue?" Michael begged.

"The thief was sure right about us finding it in a canal," Marc said. "I guess the *second forest* business was just to mislead us."

"Oh!" cried Wendy. "I forgot to tell you." She waved her arms around the wet swamp. "This is the second forest. So many of the older tree trunks are buried under the swamp soil that it's like a second forest."

"How did you know that?" Marc asked suspiciously.

Wendy smiled secretively. She didn't want to tell him she had been reading about Somerset.

"Won't somebody read the clue?" Michael pleaded once more.

Wendy took the egg from him. "Indelible ink," she said.

"Yeah," said Marc. "That could sure be Pumpelly's work."

Michael swatted his hands in the mud, spattering them all. *"Read the clue!"*

11 The Ooey, Gooey Clue

Wendy snatched the soggy egg from Michael. She wriggled her nose. "Rotten," she said.

"He sure is," Michael said.

Wendy guessed he thought she meant the thief. She read aloud:

"See the quack if you ail;
Snake root's the cure to make you well."

Wanda sneezed. "That's what we need all right — a cure for this mystery." She sneezed again.

Wendy watched Wanda closely. Her face was red and hot but she sat trembling in the puddle. "We'll look for this clue," she said gently. "You'd better go home and get some dry clothes."

"We all had," Marc agreed.

"And we'd better sneak in," Michael added.

Wendy nodded. She knew Uncle Ed would have a

fit. If he only knew all they'd been through today getting wet! But she couldn't tell him. Not yet, at least. Not till she found the "cure," which she hoped was the report.

Marc and Michael helped Wanda up. She looked like she might cry any minute. "I don't feel good," she wailed. Her knees buckled and she almost stumbled back into the water.

"I'll take her home," Marc said. "You'd better get Michael some dry clothes too."

"What for?" asked Michael, slapping his arms against his sides in a squish-splat. Little pieces of cypress and bark clung to him. His face was streaked with mud from getting the egg out of the tree stump.

"You're so muddy you look like Wanda's brother," Wendy teased.

Wanda smiled weakly. Marc put his arm around her and helped her across the yard.

Wendy let the muddy egg slide down inside the battered umbrella. Then using the umbrella as a crutch, she waded out of the thick, clammy mud.

When they reached the house, Wendy hung the umbrella on the porch rail to dry. She and Michael tiptoed around the house and peeked in the window. Uncle Ed was sitting at the table. Across from him sat Mr. Snoad. A stack of papers were scattered on the table between them. Uncle Ed had a pen in his hand. He waved it around in the air as he talked.

"Hey, Uncle Ed's signing the papers to buy the land!" Wendy said. She shivered, but with excitement instead of cold this time.

Before anyone could see them, she and Michael tore around to the back door and slipped upstairs.

The warm shower felt so good that Wendy just stood and let it flood over her like a waterfall. When she finished dressing, Michael was still splashing around in the other bathroom.

After blowing her hair about half dry, she bounded downstairs. She ran up to Uncle Ed and started to hug his neck, then stopped.

The two men sat across from each other, not speaking. The papers were now stacked neatly in the center of the table. The pen sat on top. Uncle Ed took his finger and nudged the stack to Snoad's side of the table.

The young man sighed and picked up the pen. "I might as well go on over and talk to Mrs. Sawyer about the wedding details," he said dejectedly.

Wendy looked back and forth, puzzled. But Uncle Ed just said, "Might as well," and stood up.

Wendy was curious as everything to know what was going on. But, she had learned what all kids learn pretty fast — when *not* to ask adults questions.

When Mr. Snoad left, Uncle Ed sat back down. He put his elbows on the table with his chin in his hands.

Wendy sat down across from him and looked up at him eagerly. "I saw all the papers. Were they about the land?"

"Yes," he said, looking up at her sadly.

"For the closing?" she asked hopefully.

"The closing's off," he said. "I told Snoad that with the report still missing and everything up in the air about the lake level — I just can't go through with it. I wouldn't even know how much land I'd be buying. Maybe next summer . . ."

"Next summer! But . . ." Wendy began.

"I know . . . I know," Uncle Ed said. He reached over and patted her damp, scraggly hair. "I was looking forward as much as you were to building a house and moving across the lake."

"And sailing our boat and riding the horse," Wendy added. She could see it all clearly in her mind. Was it just a dream? Could she make it come true?

"You know how things go," Uncle Ed said. "Sometimes they just don't work out."

"Couldn't anything happen to change things?" Wendy asked, afraid she already knew his answer.

"Well, the closing was supposed to be on Monday afternoon — after the lake level meeting. Snoad won't be able to get the canceled contract recorded in the courthouse before that morning. So . . . if the water level report appeared before then, I might reconsider. *But,*" he added sternly to Wendy, "you know that's not likely, so don't count on it." He rubbed her head again lightly. "Better get your reading done," he said.

Dejectedly, Wendy climbed the stairs and stretched out across the bed with her books. It had started to pour again. Two raindrop tears rolled down her cheeks and splattered on the page, blurring the words. She swatted her cheeks angrily. I'm not going to give up that easy, she thought. There's still a few days. I've got to beat that beastly thief. Maybe Snoad will help me. He'll lose a sale. Angrily she snatched up Uncle Ed's *History of Somerset Place* and began to read.

A shout from across the hall startled her. Was Michael drowning again, she muttered to herself.

Uncle Ed appeared in her doorway with a wet-headed Michael in one hand and Michael's muddy clothes in the other. "What is this? What have you kids been up to?" he demanded, not waiting for an answer. "You clean up this mess . . . and that tub," he said to Michael. He shook his head as though he didn't understand it all and walked off.

Wendy followed Michael into the bathroom. The bathtub looked like someone had made chocolate pudding in it. It was covered in a thick film of brown mud. Only the top edge above where the water had been was white, like a rim of whipped cream.

A track of muddy fingerprints climbed the wall. Wendy looked at Michael and started giggling. She was thinking of what her neat-as-a-pin grandmother would say. She laughed even harder at the thought and Michael joined in. In a minute they were both howling. Still laughing, Wendy reached down into the tub. With her forefinger, she scrawled in the mud — *clean it up*.

Just like someone had turned off a faucet, Michael stopped laughing.

Wendy scooted down the stairs. When she reached the door to the porch, she saw Uncle Ed pick up the umbrella. Wendy held her breath. The egg clue was still inside. If he saw that, he would make her explain for sure. She would even have to tell him about the canal and believing Michael and Wanda had drowned.

Then in an instant, he did it. Grumbling about kids-leaving-things-around-and-never-putting-anything-up, he opened the umbrella to shake it dry. When it shot open the egg fell *splat* on the toe of his boot. He just stood there staring at the mushy mess.

It cracked into a road map when it fell, so he didn't seem to notice the writing. Before she could warn him, Michael charged out the door and saw the egg. "The cl . . ." he began.

Wendy had to stop him before he said *clue*. "The crazy things you find in umbrellas," she blurted.

Uncle Ed just looked at her like she was crazy. He scooped up the smelly mess and marched into the house. Wendy breathed a sigh of relief. She had to launch a last ditch hunt for the report and she sure didn't need any adults in her way.

Before Uncle Ed could come back out and lecture them, she and Michael dashed to The Big House.

When they reached the mansion, they headed for the side door entrance. Marc paced back and forth across the porch looking very anxious.

"What's wrong?" Wendy asked fearfully.

Marc gave her a desperately troubled look. "Everything," he said. *"Everything!"*

12 A Mortal Fever

"Everything?" Michael repeated.

"Wanda's sick," Marc explained. "Wanda's *real* sick."

Wendy frowned. "From getting soaked in the canal?"

"I'm afraid so," Marc said.

Now Wendy paced the porch. She felt awful. She had been the one to encourage Wanda to look for the clue.

"Has she got a cold?" Michael asked.

Marc shook his head urgently. "No. Her mother says she has *a mortal fever.*"

"What's amortalfever?" Michael asked, running the words all together. Marc and Wendy giggled. Wendy figured he must think it was a disease.

"Mortal?" Wendy said suddenly. "That means fatal!"

"Well, what's afatalfever?" Michael asked.

Neither Marc nor Wendy laughed this time. "That's right," Marc said. "Deadly."

"You mean Wanda's going to die?" Michael asked, looking like he could burst into tears.

"We don't know," Marc said. "You know Mizriz Sawyer. She gets real excited about things. She might be exaggerating. I don't really know what a mortal fever is. But she's really upset . . . at us," he added, looking at Wendy.

"Because she thinks we made Wanda get all wet and sick?" Wendy guessed. Marc nodded.

"We just asked her to look for the clue — we didn't *make* her," Wendy protested, feeling like she could cry now. "She was free to choose."

"I know," Marc said, comfortingly. "We know she wanted to help."

"Have you seen her?" Michael asked eagerly. "Can we see her?"

"Her mother won't let us," Marc said. "She put her to bed in the big master bedroom on the second floor."

Suddenly Mizriz Sawyer appeared at the top of the stairs. Her large body, which always bounced jovially around the mansion seemed to sag sadly today. Her usual bright eyes were cloudy. She just stared blankly at them, then turned and went into a small room on the porch that had window panes all around.

"What's that funny room?" asked Michael. "I never saw a room on a porch before."

"It does look weird," Wendy agreed.

"You might say this was The Village's medicine cabinet," Marc said. "They would dry herbs in the windows. People would line up on the steps to get treated by the quack."

"Quack?" Michael said and laughed.

"There weren't any doctors around here. So that's what they called the person who practiced medicine," Marc explained. "When the lake would get low, the water would stagnate in the heat. Summer was even called *the sickly season.*"

"That sounds awful," Michael said.

"Well there's nothing fun about an epidemic of smallpox or yellow fever," Marc said.

"What's an epidemic?" asked Michael.

"It's when a disease spreads to a lot of people in an area," Wendy said. "That's why you have to get your booster shots each year before school starts."

"I hate that!" Michael said.

"Aw, Michael, it doesn't hurt very much," Marc said. "It's mostly in your head."

"Then how come it hurts in my arm?" Michael retorted.

"That's better than hurting somewhere else," Wendy exclaimed, rubbing her bottom.

"Or you could always try one of Pettigrew's favorite remedies — a heaping teaspoon of powdered brimstone every morning and night," Marc said.

"Brimstone!" Michael said. "Do you mean like fire and brimstone?"

"Some cure," said Wendy. "Your stomach would hurt so bad you wouldn't know if anything else hurt."

They watched Mizriz Sawyer rummage around in the small room.

"I'll bet she's trying to find something to cure Wanda," Wendy said.

"I hope it's not fire and brimstone," Michael said.

Mizriz Sawyer came out with a small parcel she held close to her bosom. Lifting her head, she looked up blankly at the children on the steps. "Go eat your lunch," she said.

"I hope Wanda will be all right," Wendy said earnestly. But Mizriz Sawyer marched on by and back into the house.

Forlornly, the group headed for the kitchen. Mizriz Sawyer usually kept everything spotless. But today, the breakfast dishes were still scattered around.

She had made sandwiches and they were spread around on paper towels as though she had just tossed them there. Snoad was sitting at the end of the table drinking coffee. He looked as glum as they did.

Hopping up on the stool beside him, Michael began to eat like a beast. Instead of sitting down, Marc started cleaning up the dishes.

Wendy helped. She felt Snoad staring at her while she worked. Finally he spoke. "I'm sorry about your Uncle's land deal falling through," he said, looking as if he were more sorry for himself than her.

"Me, too," she said glumly, wishing she could tell him that all might not be lost yet.

"I just don't know where Allison and I will live now after we're married," he said. "I really counted on selling all the lots on that side of the lake so we could use my commissions to buy the last one for ourselves. I grew up around here, and I don't want to leave. This lake level mess has caused a lot of problems. I haven't sold a lot on the lake all year," he said sadly.

"Oh yeah," Marc said. "Your wedding's this weekend."

He made it sound like a funeral, Wendy thought.

She wished she hadn't even thought of the word *funeral* — not while Wanda had a mortal fever, whatever that was.

The door opened and Mizriz Sawyer came into the room. She looked at the clean counter and smiled wanly.

"Please tell us how Wanda is," Wendy begged.

"Better," she said, with a big sigh. She turned to Snoad. "Yes, the wedding's this weekend and we have a lot to do. Like make a wedding cake!" She poured a big glass of milk and put it on a tray.

"Is that for Wanda?" Wendy asked.

Mizriz Sawyer nodded, not looking up.

"Can we take it up to her?" Wendy begged. *"Please,"* she added.

The woman shook her head and smiled. "All right," she said. "But don't make a rumpus. Just stay a minute."

Wendy jumped up, almost turning her stool over. Michael abandoned his half-eaten sandwich. And Marc shoved the last of the clean dishes in the cupboard. Wendy grabbed the tray and they hurried out of the kitchen.

In the downstairs hall they passed Mr. Pumpelly who warned them not to spill the milk on the carpet. Wendy just frowned at him and kept walking.

By the time she reached the top of the stairs, Marc and Michael were already tapping on the master bedroom door. A weak voice squeaked, *"Come in,"* and the boys cracked the door open and slipped inside. Wendy followed and put the tray of milk beside Wanda's bed.

"How's your amortalfever?" Michael asked.

Wanda gave him a funny look. "I feel okay," she said softly. "I just had a bad cold."

"But your mother made us think you were going to d . . ." Marc began.

Quickly, Wendy interrupted " . . . Think you were going to be well real soon."

"I do feel better," Wanda said, but Wendy could tell she still felt pretty groggy and tired. "I want to help you find the next clue," she added weakly.

"Oh no!" Wendy insisted, "You stay right here and get well. If we find anything, you'll be the first to know."

"I'm so glad you've come," Wanda said. "I've been trying to get Mama to tell you, but she just says I'm hall . . . hallu . . ."

"Hallucinating?" Marc asked.

"Yes," said Wanda. "She just says I only think it's true, but that it really isn't. That it's just the fever. But I know it isn't!"

They all moved closer to the bed. Wanda's dark little face looked lost against the fat white pillows and blankets.

"What's true?" Wendy begged.

Wanda pulled her arm out from under the covers and pointed at the ceiling. "There's something in the attic," she said. "I heard it."

13 A Mysterious Moan

"Maybe it's just Mr. Pumpelly sneaking around again," Marc said.

Wendy had an idea. "When was the last time you heard something?" she asked.

"Right before you came in," Wanda said. "That's why I jumped when you knocked on the door."

Wendy looked at Marc. "Mr. Pumpelly was downstairs then," she said.

"Yeah, he fussed at us not to spill the milk," Michael remembered.

"What does the noise sound like?" asked Marc.

"It's a moan," Wanda said, slipping down further under the blankets until they covered the bottom of her chin. "An *ooooo* kind of moan — over and over and over."

"We'd better check that out," Wendy said.

Wanda shook the covers off of her chin. "Mama said we'd better not go up there anymore."

"How did she know we'd been in the attic?" Marc asked.

Wanda slid back down beneath the covers again. "I guess I told her when I was hallu . . ."

"Hallucinating," Wendy said. "No wonder your mother was so ill with us earlier."

"That spooky sound makes me afraid to sleep here by myself at night," Wanda said.

Marc's face lit up. "I know," he said. "We'll make you an aspidity bag."

"What's that?" asked Michael.

"It's a combination of herbs in a little pouch," Marc said. "You wear it around your neck and it's supposed to ward off evil. You won't have to be afraid of anything."

Wendy knew that was all a bunch of hocus pocus. But she thought it was nice of Marc to try and make Wanda feel safer about staying alone at night in this big, dark room — especially with something moaning overhead. She'd be scared herself.

"We'll be around more now that your mom will let us see you," Wendy said. "And if we find anything out about the clue, you'll be the first to know."

"I'll stay here and play whist with Wanda for a while," Michael offered. "If she feels like it," he added.

Wanda popped up out of the covers. She grabbed a deck of cards from under her pillow.

Marc laughed. "Where did you hallucinate those cards from?" he asked.

"Well, besides being scary, it gets boring to stay here all by yourself waiting to get well," Wanda pouted.

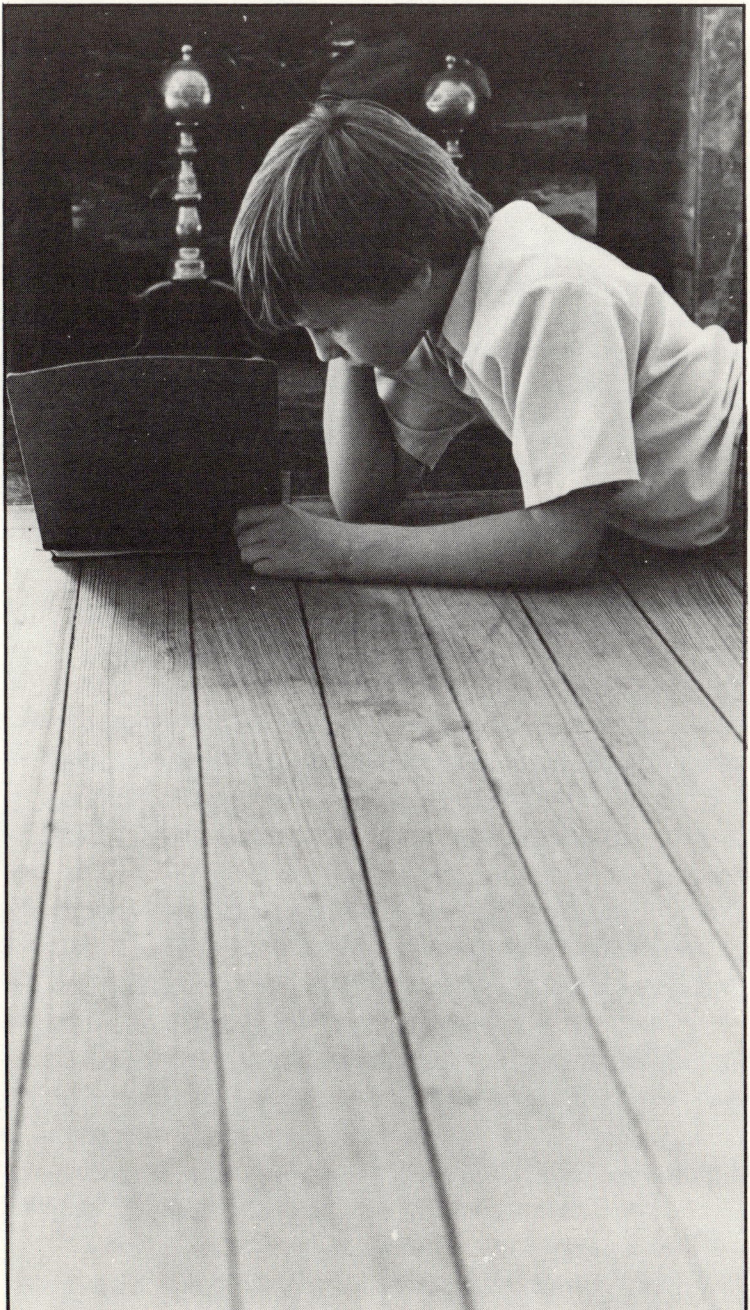

A Mysterious Moan

Wendy picked up the empty glass and the tray. She and Marc hurried back to the kitchen to get some string for the aspidity bag.

"What — or who — do you think the sound Wanda heard could be?" Marc asked.

"That's a good question," said Wendy. "It could be the thief, or the beast, or one of the Somerset ghosts, or Mr. Pumpelly, or just Wanda's imagination, or . . ."

"'All right . . . all right," Marc said.

"Well," Wendy said, "the only way we'll find out is to go up in the attic."

She pushed the kitchen door open with her foot.

"Wanda's much better!" she said. "Michael's playing cards with her now."

Mizriz Sawyer and Snoad were talking about the upcoming wedding. "We haven't had a wedding in years," she said. "It'll be just like Master Collins when he brought his bride to Somerset."

"Except that he got to stay," Snoad grumbled.

"You and Allison will find a place to live," she told Snoad.

Wendy slumped against the counter. In all her relief over Wanda being all right, she had almost forgotten about her main problem. Sure Snoad would find a place to live around here all right. But she would have to go back to Atlanta. They hadn't even found the report yet, and they had had a new clue from the canal for a whole day now.

The two adults started planning where people would sit, and what they would wear, and all the other dull stuff about the wedding. Wendy only wanted to hear about the food. Phooey with the rest.

Marc edged toward the door and she followed. They went out and he showed her the string he had found in a drawer.

"Where are you going to get the herbs?" Wendy asked.

"Can't you guess?" he said, heading up the side stairs.

Wendy had only followed him a few steps when she realized where he was going. "Of course," she said, "the medicine room."

The small room on the porch made her think of a potting shed or the tiny curbside flower shops in big cities. It smelled funny inside. There were nails to hang herbs on and drawers under the wooden counter for medicines.

Marc reached into one drawer and a funny look came over his face. He slowly pulled his hand back out and shoved his tightly closed fist toward Wendy.

14 A Blue Clue

Wendy pried his fingers open and saw a blue egg. "It's about time we had a little luck on this case," she said.

"It certainly is," Marc agreed, turning the new clue over. He read:

*"If you want the report in your hands . . .
Look in the place they call Rich Lands."*

"The report!" Wendy squealed. "It tells us where the report is!"

"Do you believe it?" Marc asked.

"I *have* to believe," Wendy stressed. "At least I have to check it out. Even though it seems like we keep running into a dead end."

Suddenly Wendy understood. "You think you know who the thief is, don't you?" she said.

Now Marc leaned lazily back against the counter.

He yawned. Then he scratched his head and looked out the window like he had forgotten Wendy was there. She felt like she could clobber him. But there was nothing to do but be patient with this unbearable boy, she thought.

"Well," Marc finally said, "it could be someone who just happened to have fixed the eggs anyway, *and* who knew when Uncle Ed was going to hide them, *and* where, and . . ."

"Mr. Pumpelly knew all that," Wendy said angrily, snapping a strange, knobby herb root in half.

"He didn't fix the eggs," Marc reminded her.

"Of course not, Mizriz . . ." Wendy began, then stopped. Her mouth hung open. *"You don't think . . ."* she began again.

Marc shuffled his feet and kicked some stray herbs around the floor. She could tell he hated to accuse someone like Wanda's mother of being a thief. He sighed and said softly, "You know she feels strongly about changing the lake. She truly thinks controlling the water level will make awful things happen at Somerset. More drownings or hangings or something."

"She's just superstitious," Wendy defended her.

"I think she probably ran across the report on your uncle's desk when she was cleaning and thought it was fate or something," Marc said.

"You mean like she really should take it — like it wouldn't be wrong," Wendy said.

"Yes," said Marc. "She would think it was her duty — to save the lake, or something crazy like that."

"But what about the clues?" Wendy asked.

"Well, she knew how determined you were to find

the report. I guess she thought a bunch of hoax clues would keep you busy and out of the way until the date passed for them to vote on the report."

"She never suspected I'd get the world involved in helping me," Wendy guessed.

"Of course not," said Marc. "That's probably why she was so angry about Wanda getting sick."

"Yeah," Wendy said. "She wasn't mad at us. She was mad at herself. If she hadn't taken the report, Wanda wouldn't have ended up out in the rain looking for a clue."

Marc laid the egg on the counter. "I don't think she meant for us to find this clue," he suggested. "I think she just hid it here when she got Wanda's medicine, never thinking we'd find it."

Wendy felt very sad. She never suspected that someone as nice as Mizriz Sawyer would steal something. She sure didn't like thinking her friend's mother was a thief.

"We told Wanda she'd be the first to know about another clue," Marc reminded Wendy.

Suddenly Wendy jumped off the counter. "But what about Pumpelly?" she said.

Marc shook his head. "I don't know," he said. "He feels as strongly as Mizriz Sawyer about leaving the lake level alone . . ."

". . . And he had the indelible markers," Wendy reminded him.

". . . And he's a sneaky person, anyway," Marc added.

". . . The kind who would hide an egg in here to make it look like someone else did it," Wendy said.

They just stood there and stared at each other.

How could they know who the thief was? Suddenly another thought occurred to Wendy. "The thief is either Mizriz Sawyer, Mr. Pumpelly . . . or," she added, "the moan in the attic!"

15 Rich Lands

Sunday morning was sunny and hot. Wendy sat on the porch of The Gate House and frowned. It was the day of the wedding. Everyone was happy and excited. Except her.

She only had twenty-four hours left to solve the mystery, and things were more mysterious than ever. Not only that, no one wanted to help her anymore.

Uncle Ed was resigned to the fact that he was not going to buy the land. Snoad was too busy getting married to care about where he lived. Marc was excited over the horse race today. Wanda was up and about, but her mother was keeping her close to the house. And Michael was too busy licking leftover frosting out of bowls and off of spoons.

Wendy was on her own. And it sure seemed hopeless.

She walked slowly towards the mansion, scuffing the toes of her freshly polished white shoes against the brick walk with each step.

Everything in The Village was fresh and green. But it was too hot, Wendy thought, scratching her shoulders where the white ribbon ties of her sundress tickled her mosquito bites. Her shoes felt like cereal boxes on her feet after going barefoot so much.

Inside the mansion, Mr. Pumpelly was arranging flowers. He kept putting them in different places. He would step back and look at them sourly with his hand under his chin, his eyes squinted, and his head thrown back. Then he would mumble and frown and snatch the flowers up and prance off to another room and do the same thing.

Mizriz Sawyer was in the kitchen putting the final touches on the big wedding cake. Michael followed her every step.

In a place as isolated and as quiet as Somerset, a wedding was still a big event, just as it had been in the Collins' day. Everyone had come from all around. It would be a true *Tuskarora frolik,* just as Mizriz Sawyer had said.

Across from the mansion, Mr. Walker was setting up for the horse races. The wide expanse of The Lawn was still misty with morning dew.

Wendy wanted to go in the master bedroom to see if she could hear the moan, but Allison was there with a seamstress adjusting her wedding gown.

Wendy crossed the canal to talk to Mr. Walker. He was draping colorful streamers of flags between the big oak trees. When he saw Wendy he smiled at her.

Wendy scruffed her foot across the base of a tree and tried to ask casually, "Is there a place around here called *Rich Lands?*"

"Oh, yes," Mr. Walker said. She tripped over the root in surprise.

He pointed toward the path that led to the Pettigrew Place. The path where she had first seen the beast.

"That's one name for Bonarva-Pettigrew's old homeplace," he said. "Ebenezer Pettigrew was a hard-working, religious man. He didn't think much of the Collins' fancy ways. So they were always having petty feuds over something."

"You mean here they were the only neighbors they had for miles and miles and they argued?" Wendy said.

Mr. Walker laughed. "Well, they both changed some pretty worthless land to good farms. But Pettigrew did it without the money and slaves that Collins had."

"Good for him," Wendy said.

"Of course they didn't always fight," Mr. Walker said. "Mr. Collins liked to read aloud and the Pettigrew children would come and listen. Mrs. Pettigrew even came to listen," he added, looking down at Wendy.

"Why would she come?" Wendy asked.

"Well," said Mr. Walker, "apparently she never learned to read."

Wendy squinted and looked away. Just because she wasn't crazy about reading didn't mean she didn't think everyone should know how.

Mr. Walker handed Wendy the end of a streamer to tie down. "And if you think this wedding is something, you should hear about Christmas celebrations the Collinses used to have!"

"Yeah!" said Wendy. Christmas was her favorite holiday. "What did they do?"

"Well, Christmas was one of the few holidays that the slaves got to participate in," he said. "They had a special celebration that they called *Koonering.*"

"What in the world was that?" asked Wendy.

Mr. Walker explained. "One of the slaves would come to the front door of the mansion all dressed up in costume so only his eyes and mouth showed. He would dance in front of the master of the house hoping he would toss coins. I think it was a ceremony based on those of their African ancestors."

"Sounds like begging," Wendy said.

"Well, they did call the costumed person the *ragman,*" Mr. Walker said.

Wendy let her streamer flutter to the ground. "Why?" she asked. "What's his costume?"

Mr. Walker looked up at her, surprised. "Rags, of course, layers and layers of furry rags. He would look like a regular beast," he said and laughed.

Wendy didn't laugh. She just turned and ran across the lawn. She finally stopped at the path that led to Rich Lands. Could the beast have anything to do with the stolen report, she wondered. She took a few steps toward the path when a voice from behind stopped her.

"Aren't you going to watch the races?" Marc asked.

"Yeah," Michael said behind him, "Marc's going to be in the first race. Wanna place a bet?"

"Gambling's illegal," Wanda protested.

"Not at horse races," Michael argued.

"I bet he's going to fall off," Wendy said irritably.

"Thanks a lot," said Marc.

Mr. Walker hurried by. "You kids help," he ordered. He was busy picking up stray limbs from the grassy track. They all stooped to help him.

By the time Wendy had finished picking up her share of sticks and rocks, she looked up and saw that the guests were arriving.

Ladies in long dresses filled the wide porch. Children played with colorful sailboats in the rippling canal. Men jaunted across the bridge with their horses. It was like looking back in time, Wendy thought. It was probably the most festive thing she'd ever seen. But she didn't feel festive at all.

A group of horses lined up for the first race. Wendy watched Marc mount his horse. She was really jealous. If she just had Charley Horse, she could be in the race too. And she'd beat him!

Horses and riders pranced around the track once for show. The spectators across the canal cheered and applauded. When they reached the starting line, Mr. Walker shot a blank bullet into the air and the horses flew.

Marc got off to the best start. He was out in front from the beginning. Wendy found herself pulling for him, in spite of herself.

He came charging around the first turn, way ahead of the others. Then suddenly, as Wendy watched, the most awful thing she could imagine happened.

Like this book?
See the coupons in the back
to order other
HISTORY MYSTERY$_{TM}$ books!

16 The Bad, Old Beast

Marc's horse tripped. He tumbled forward and landed against a big oak tree. His horse kept running.

Wendy screamed and ran toward him. Because she was so close, she was the first to reach him. He looked up at her in a daze and raised his hand to rub his head. But his arm fell slowly to the ground. Just before he fainted he looked at Wendy with glazed eyes and said, as he had earlier, "Thanks a lot — thanks . . . a . . . lot . . ."

Suddenly everyone was crowding around her. Mr. Walker grabbed her by the arm. "Move . . . move . . . please . . ." he shouted. "Give him air . . ."

Wendy backed away from Marc and the group of people. Suddenly she fell backwards on the grass. She had tripped on a big log. She couldn't believe it. That was what caused Marc to fall.

Then she understood. He had seen her picking up sticks. He must have thought she had left this one on purpose to trip him, knowing he'd probably be the first one to make the turn. She sat down on the log and put her face in her hands.

Michael and Wanda ran up. "Is Marc all right?" they asked together.

"I don't know," Wendy said, near tears. "He thinks I did it. He thinks I put the log there."

"No . . . nooooo!" Wanda squealed. "The beast did it!"

"We saw him," Michael agreed.

"When we were coming up the road," Wanda explained. "We were late for the race. We saw the beast go off in the woods."

"It was carrying a log in its hands," Michael said.

Wendy looked up at them both in disbelief. Her head throbbed as much as she figured Marc's probably did. It was one thing to steal a report, she thought, but another thing to hurt someone.

Wendy jumped up off the log. Marc had been taken inside already and the races were fixing to start up again. Some men were scouting the field once more to check for logs or rocks.

She gave Wanda and Michael a shove toward the house. "Let's go," she ordered. "We've got to figure out who this beast is and what it wants before someone gets killed or something."

By the time they reached the house, Marc had been put to bed in the master bedroom. Mizriz Sawyer and Mr. Walker were both coming down the stairs, shaking their heads and talking in low tones about the accident.

They waited behind the parlor door until the adults went by, then they slipped up the stairs and into the

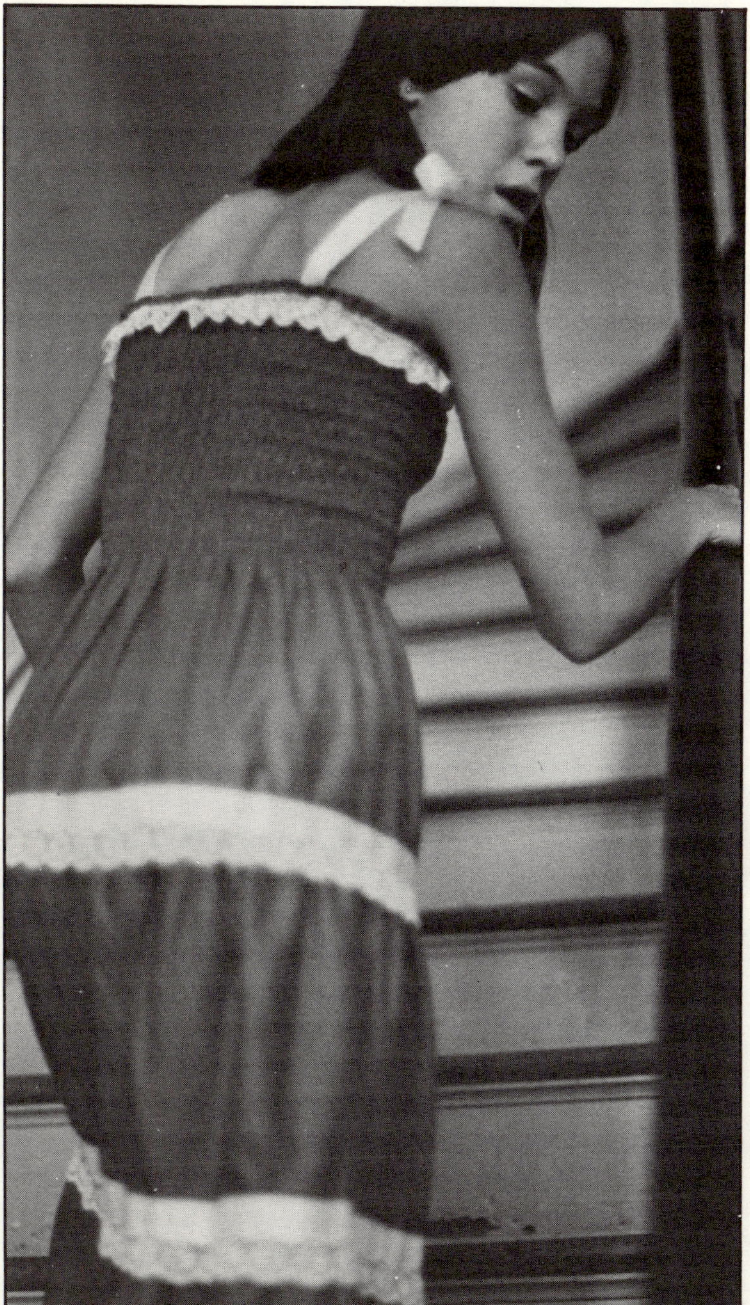

bedroom.

Marc was propped up in the bed like Wanda had been. But sitting on top of his head was an ice pack.

"You look like a king with a crown on in that big, old bed," Michael said.

Marc didn't speak. He just glared at Wendy.

"She didn't do it!" Wanda said.

Marc frowned at Wanda even harder.

"She didn't," Michael said. "It was the beast . . . we saw him."

"Sure," moaned Marc. "You're just trying to defend her."

"No . . ." begged Wanda. "We saw the beast run away with a log in his hands."

While they were arguing over who believed who, Wendy suddenly motioned for them to hush. "Listen," she begged.

They were all very still. After a minute Marc lifted the ice pack from his head and leaned forward. "I hear it," he said.

"The moan!" Michael said, and moved closer to the bed.

"That's what I heard before," Wanda whispered. "That's the same sound."

"And it's coming from the attic," Marc said.

Wendy turned on her heels and headed for the door.

"Where are you going?" asked Marc.

"Where else? . . . to the attic," she said determinedly.

"But Mama said we weren't allowed to go up there," Wanda reminded her.

"Well, *we're* not going," Wendy said, angrily.

"Only I am. I'll be the only one to get in trouble."

Michael and Wanda looked relieved.

"But this stupid beast, or whatever it is, has caused enough trouble," Wendy said. "I'm going to find out what it is."

Marc stared at her. But she just stared back. She thought he was a beast for thinking she would do anything as awful as hurt someone ... anyone. She marched out of the room.

Wendy hurried to the end of the hall before she could lose her courage. She remembered being half scared out of her wits the last time she had been in the attic. And now she was going up there by herself voluntarily. *You're brave,* Wendy Long, she told herself. *Brave, but dumb.*

Sneaking silently up the skinny steps, Wendy reached for the door knob. Something breathing behind her loudly caused her to hold her own breath. She felt trapped between a beast in the attic and a spooky unknown behind her on the stairs. Wendy whirled around. Wanda and Michael crouched on the steps below her. One round white face. One round black face. And two identical grins.

"Marc told us to come with you," Wanda said.

"He said we could run for help if you need it," Michael added.

Wendy sighed twice in relief. Once to see that it was only Wanda and Michael breathing down her neck. And again, to know that Marc must believe that she was telling the truth.

"Well, be quiet," she said gruffly, glad to have them along. They snuck up the rest of the steps and huddled right behind her. She reached for the knob again, and just as she opened the door, a voice from beneath the stairs shouted, "What do you kids think you're doing?"

17 A Weird Wedding

The three of them gasped and whipped around. Mr. Pumpelly stood at the bottom of the stairs with his hands on his hips. Wendy couldn't help but notice that he wore a brown suit with a brown shirt. Perched on his head was a brown hat with a little brown feather. He also had a very brown look on his face that Wendy didn't like.

"I thought you children were told to stay away from the attic," he barked up the steps.

"We heard a . . ." Michael began.

Wendy punched him in the back so hard he fell down one step. Then she grabbed him by the back of his shirt to catch him. "We heard a noise," she said. She knew that they'd better not say they heard a beast moaning.

"Well, I've got my wallpaper samples up there," Mr. Pumpelly whined, "and I do not want them to be disturbed, so come down this instant."

Reluctantly, Wendy closed the attic door. They trudged down the stairs. Michael wouldn't even stand up. He just bumped, bumped, bumped down the stairs on his bottom. Mr. Pumpelly glared at him like he thought that was awful. Wendy and Wanda giggled in spite of themselves.

Huffing and puffing, Mr. Pumpelly led the way downstairs. Wendy was afraid that he was going to take them to Mizriz Sawyer or Uncle Ed. But when they reached the library, he just turned and sneered at them and went into the parlor to finish arranging his flowers.

"Plump belly!" Michael said under his breath.

"Beast!" said Wanda, not as quietly.

"Shhh!" warned Wendy, staring at the man stooped over a low table. He surely did look like a big brown beast, she thought.

They went into the kitchen.

"Mysteries make me hungry," Michael said, and Wendy realized that it had been a long time since breakfast. Mizriz Sawyer was busy putting the finishing touches on the wedding cake.

"Oh, Mother!" said Wanda.

"It's beautiful!" Wendy said. The three layer cake was shaped like The Big House. It was covered with pale yellow icing. The windows and balconies were white. Green icing vines climbed up the side walls. A figure of a bride and groom stood on the front porch.

Wendy thought it was the most beautiful cake she had ever seen. "You could make a lot of money doing fancy cakes like that in Atlanta," she said.

Mizriz Sawyer just smiled and kept smoothing out little wrinkles of frosting. "I like making my cakes right here," she said.

"Can I have a bite of chimney?" Michael asked.

"Don't you dare touch this cake, chile," Mizriz Sawyer hollered, rapping his knuckles with a spatula. Frosting stuck to Michael's hand and he licked his fingers in delight. Wendy and Wanda looked at him jealously. Mizriz Sawyer stuck the spatula into the bowl again and swiped it across their fingers held in the air.

"Delicious!" Wanda said, smacking her lips.

"When do we eat?" asked Wendy.

"Soon," Mizriz Sawyer said. "You all better go and get dressed. The wedding's in one hour. Poor Miss Allison's just beside herself," she said, shaking the spatula again and splattering icing in her hair. "Mr. Snoad hasn't been seen all afternoon," Mizriz Sawyer said. "But I suspect he'll be back any minute."

"Can we take a sample of icing to Marc?" Wanda asked.

Her mother plopped a big blob of yellow frosting on a small paper plate and handed it to Wanda. "Now scat! All of you."

They hurried back up the stairs, trying to avoid Mr. Pumpelly. Marc glared at them when they came in. "Where have you been?" he said. "I thought something must have gotten you. I didn't hear the moaning anymore."

"Something did get us," Wendy said, telling him about Mr. Pumpelly.

"He's a suspicious character," Marc agreed. "And this is suspicious too," he added, taking the plate of icing from Michael. The blob was full of fingerprints.

Suddenly the grandfather clock in the downstairs

hall chimed. "Shhh," said Wendy. "Oh, phooey, it's not a moan. It's the clock. You guys are supposed to be getting dressed for the wedding."

"Why can't we wear our cutoff jeans to the stupid wedding?" Michael grumbled as they left.

While she waited for the other kids to dress, Wendy watched the mansion fill with people. The ladies looked beautiful in their straw hats with flowing ribbons. All the men had on white suits and pastel-colored shirts.

Wendy had to admit that Mr. Pumpelly had done a beautiful job with the flower arrangements. There was something lovely on every table. It seemed like outdoors had come inside. What looked like a million candles reflected in mirrors and vases and the ripply window panes.

The big wedding cake sat on a table in the hall surrounded by china plates and shining silver that glistened in the candlelight. When they passed by the cake, Wendy saw Michael start to run his finger down the side of the house. She snatched his hand away and he stuck his tongue out at her.

They finally found Wanda on the front porch. She and Wendy admired each other's frilly dresses.

"You do look nice," a voice said shyly behind them.

It was Marc. Wendy couldn't believe he said that or that he was dressed up. She blushed. "Well, I haven't seen you two guys look this clean all summer," she said.

"Michael even combed his hair!" Wanda teased.

Just as the peach-colored sun sank into the lavender lake, the sound of the antique piano filled the air. Slowly everyone filed inside the candlelit house. Uncle Ed motioned for them to go and stand on the staircase where they could see over the adults' heads.

From her perch on the curved stairs, Wendy could see the people and the room and the candlelight reflected in the old convex mirror over the mantle. The scene looked funny all crowded into a round circle with everything in the center fat and on the edges thin. It looked like the pictures Michael's mother made with her fish eye lens.

The front door opened and Allison waltzed into the hallway. Wanda tapped Wendy on the shoulder. "Doesn't she look beautiful?"

Wendy nodded. Her dress was like a fabric wedding cake. A billowing veil streamed behind her. She floated down the long hall. Once, before she turned to go into the parlor, she looked up at them and smiled.

When the music stopped, Wendy looked out of the window at the last glimmer of sunlight. She could barely make out the far horizon of the lake, where she could have lived. It looked like that would never happen now. It was Sunday night and she was running out of time, and ideas, and help.

She wondered if Mr. Snoad felt as bad as she did. She looked around. She hadn't seen him anywhere. And he was the groom! Mr. Pumpelly began to play the wedding refrain again. Allison's smile melted into a frown.

Suddenly, the candles flickered as though a gust of wind had sneaked in a window. The front door burst open. And there in the doorway, in front of them, stood the beast.

18 Help!

Instantly, there was chaos and confusion. Mizriz Sawyer, who was standing in the library door, threw up her apron and exlaimed, "Kooner! It's John Kooner!"

The raggedy beast stalked toward the steps. Wendy could see that the brown bundle of monster was more like layers and layers of rags instead of hair. It looked like a fur mummy coming unwrapped everywhere.

Guests crowded the doors of the library and parlor and drawing room. When they saw the beast, they began to squeal. Some dashed out of the front door.

The men grabbed fire pokers from the fireplace hearth. The beast took a few steps nearer to the stairs. Wendy and Marc and Wanda and Michael sat frozen on the steps as though they were part of a cake or something and couldn't move.

The beast looked even larger in the candlelight. It

threw a huge, hairy shadow down the long hall and up the stairs over them.

Suddenly the men charged at the beast. It ran toward the stairs, bumping against the furniture and knocking the wedding cake over. Its brown eyes stared straight into Wendy's. All she could think of was that the eyes didn't look like a beast's at all, but very sad and confused.

Then suddenly the beast did something that even Wendy would have never expected. With a leap it charged up the stairs and scrambled around the four children, the raggedy body dragging over them. Wanda and Michael screamed. Wendy saw Marc grab for the beast's back but lose his grip and fall backwards.

Wendy just ducked as the beast passed her, then she turned and ran up the steps after it.

Wendy thought the men would be right behind her, but in the dark and the confusion they couldn't get over the startled kids sprawled on the stairs.

Wendy tore up the stairs to the second floor. Her heart beat like those of a thousand runners in a race. She was afraid and angry; scared yet curious about this strange beast.

The raggedy thing didn't even stop on the second floor. Just as Wendy expected, it bound up the next flight of stairs and disappeared into the attic. She followed it as fast as she could. Without thinking, she dashed through the small attic door.

It was like falling into a haunted house at the fair. Everything was pitch black. No candlelight. No moonlight. She froze. In a second her eyes adjusted and she could see a strange, red glow in the room. It was just

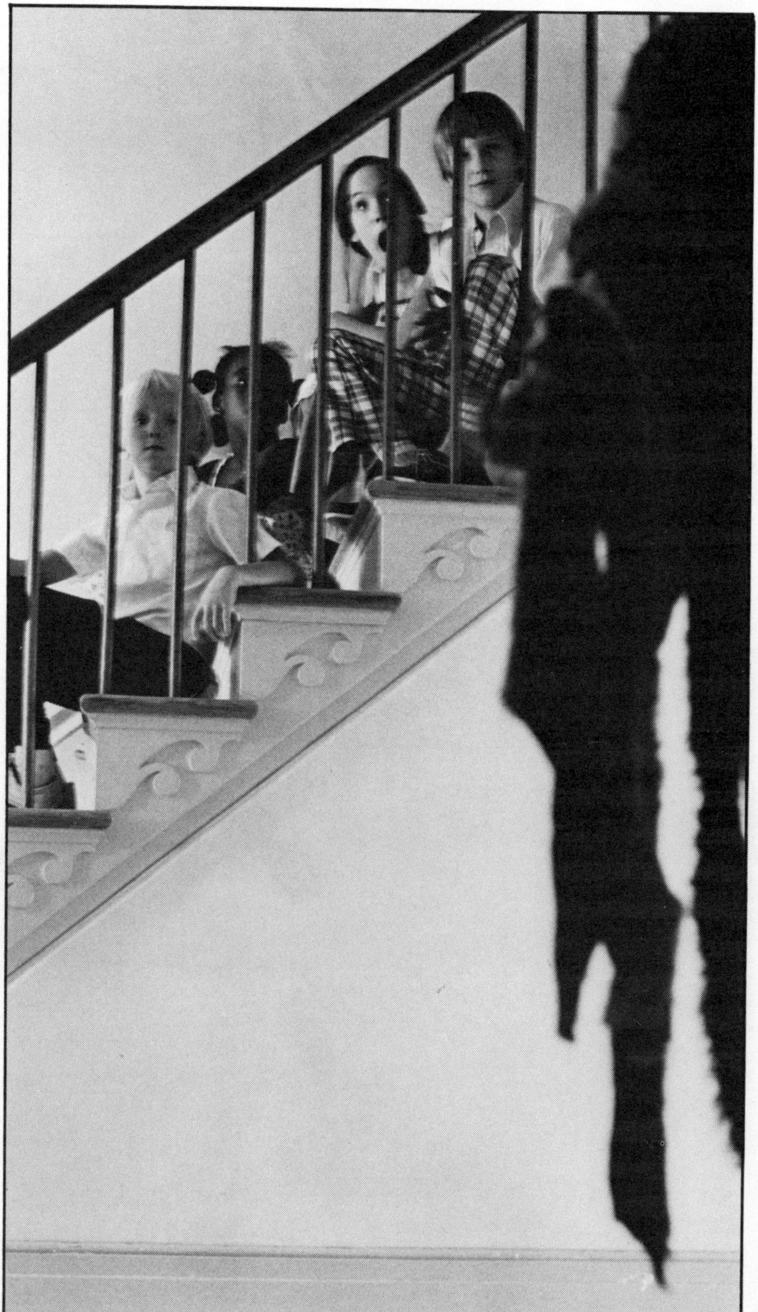

enough light to see that the cooling room door was open.

She could feel her courage fading fast. But she couldn't give up now, she thought. Walking quickly to the cooling room, she stepped inside, her arms clinched by her sides. Suddenly she heard the sound of a moan like they had heard earlier from the master bedroom.

She had to get out of here!

In the darkness she got turned around. Instead of the cooling room door, she grasped the door knob to the little garret room and went inside.

As soon as she stepped into the room she knew she had done the wrong thing. This was the end of the line. There was no place for the beast to run from here. It had to be in the room with her.

With a woosh, she felt the rags graze her arm as the beast passed her and disappeared into the red glow. Running after him, she tripped. She hoped she was hallucinating. But no, it was true — she was hanging half in and half out of the house from the third floor window.

19 A Chase Through the Swamp

Just when Wendy thought she would fall or faint, she felt a hand grab her dress and yank her back inside.

She turned and grasped the hand gratefully. "Marc!" she said. "Look! The lake is on fire!"

They both stared out the window into the reddish glow. A swamp fire burned along the edge of the lake. It reflected bright red in the water, and pink in the hazy mist of the warm spring night.

Wendy saw men running toward the fire. There was a thud below them.

"The beast!" Marc said, as they watched the raggedy outline of the figure cross the balcony below them.

"It's going across the canal," Wendy said.

"Well, we can't get out this way," Marc said.

"Let's go off the master bedroom balcony," Wendy suggested. "It's not as high."

Together they charged into the cooling room and bumped smack into Wanda and Michael.

"You scared us to death!" Wanda squealed.

Marc and Wendy just ran on, never speaking.

Since everyone was helping put out the fire or watching from the front porch, there was no one on the second floor.

They slipped into the master bedroom. Marc threw open a window and they scooted out onto the balcony. He went down first. Wendy helped Wanda and Michael over the side. Then she jumped and they all ran toward the bridge over the canal.

As she charged past the others, Wendy could hear Uncle Ed calling for her to stop.

Into the dark woods she plunged with the others at her heels. She had one last glimpse of the beast before the thick canopy of trees blotted out all light from the fire. Wendy ran as fast as she could in the darkness, determined to catch the beast.

A limb caught in her dress and stopped her. She yanked it loose, then stood still for a moment. It was deadly quiet except for the muffled sound of the firefighters in the distance.

She couldn't hear the others. She figured they must all be walking on different paths, since there were so many here by the lake between Somerset and the Pettigrew Place. For all she knew, they were walking around in circles and would bump into each other at any step.

Suddenly there was the crack of thunder and a flash of lightning. In the brief second of light, she saw something a little ahead of her.

Taking off her shoes she began to run again. The

ground was soft beneath her feet, then damp, then watery. She stopped. The silence was pierced by a splash and a garbled cry of *"Help!"*

Wendy stood still. She didn't know what to do. What if it were the beast? What if it was a trick? She started to turn and run. But, she thought, what if the splash was Marc? Or Wanda? Or Michael?

She held tight to a tree limb. Then, like a pop of thunder, she broke the limb off and called into the darkness ahead of her. "Where are you?"

"Help . . . help!" a voice answered. She moved forward with the limb in front of her.

A flash of lightning showed her what she feared. A few steps ahead in an old canal was the beast. It was thrashing around desperately. Even in the split second of light, Wendy saw the pleading brown eyes.

She thrust the limb out in front of her. "Here, take this!" she called. She stooped down and tried to stretch the limb farther out. Her feet began to slide on the muddy edge of the bank. Rain flooded down on them now and the beast kept sinking into the murky water.

She knew people who were drowning could panic. The beast could pull her in if she got much closer, then she couldn't help at all.

Suddenly something grabbed the side of her dress. It was Marc. "I see him," he called, above the noisy rainfall. "Can you get closer now?"

Without speaking, she inched her way slowly forward.

Then, the beast snatched the limb. It grabbed so hard that it pulled her into the water up to her knees. Another step and she would be over her head. Marc tugged on her dress. Next . . . and she could feel it more than she could hear it . . . the dress began to rip.

She felt Marc's hand slip away. The beast was pulling her down into the water.

And then, someone grabbed her tightly around the waist.

"Uncle Ed!" she cried. "Help the beast! He's drowning."

Uncle Ed took the limb and pulled the beast up out of the water.

Wendy plopped down into the mud by Marc and stood staring at the dripping, raggedy beast. At least the bottom part was beast. The top rags had washed away and a man's wet head stuck out.

"Mr. Snoad!" Wendy cried in shock and fell back into the swamp, speechless.

20 Bless the Beast

It was two in the morning, but Wendy had never felt more awake. She and Marc and Wanda and Michael sat on the sofa in the parlor in front of a small fire Mr. Walker had made so they could dry out.

Mizriz Sawyer had sliced them each a gigantic piece of the wedding cake that didn't fall over. It was just as delicious as it had looked. Even Mr. Pumpelly didn't fuss about the crumbs Michael was spilling on the floor.

Mr. Snoad sat in a chair by the fire. He had put on dry clothes, but his hair was still wet. Allison stood behind him, her eyes red from crying.

Everyone looked at him like he was a sneaky, old toad.

"I'm so sorry," Snoad was saying. He hung his head. "I didn't mean to scare everyone so bad and cause so much trouble." Allison patted him on the shoulder as though she were trying to understand.

Wendy was trying to understand too. Trying to figure out why he would steal the lake level report and pretend to be a beast. She could see from the stern looks on Uncle Ed and Mr. Walker's faces that they didn't feel very understanding.

"I just wanted Allison and me to live across the lake so much," he said. "It means everything to me. I can't imagine living anywhere else in the world."

Wendy took another bite of cake. She could understand that, she thought. She felt that way about Somerset Place too.

"But when you stole that report, you jeopardized everyone's right to enjoy Lake Phelps," Mr. Walker said.

"That's right," Uncle Ed agreed. "You've messed up the chance for Wendy and me to live here together. And you know how bad she wanted that!"

Snoad looked at Wendy and shook his head. "Boy, do I know!" he said. "I thought I could just hide the report over at the old Pettigrew Place until the date for the decision was over," he said. "With the report gone, I thought people would give in and buy their land — instead of cancel their contract like you did — and I would have the money to buy the last lot for me and Allison."

"But I never knew Wendy would track me down," Snoad said. "I knew if I didn't do something to steer her away from Rich Lands, she might find the report."

"Is that when you stole our Easter eggs and made the clues?" Wanda asked.

Snoad nodded and Wanda looked at him like she thought he was still a beast.

"And you found an old John Kooner costume and

dressed up like a beast," Marc said.

Snoad hung his head.

"But what about Marc?" Wendy said. "You didn't have to hurt him at the horse race to get me to stop looking," she said. "And he thought I did it!"

Snoad looked puzzled.

"Did what?" he asked.

"You know," Michael said. "Put the log there for his horse to trip over."

"Oh no," Allison said. "I'm sure . . ."

Mr. Pumpelly cleared his throat and interrupted her. "The log was there," he said. "I was out in the field pulling wild flowers for the arrangements. I looked up when I heard the race start and saw the log. Didn't you see me jump out to get it?" he asked.

Wendy looked at Wanda and Michael. "You *did* see a brown beast," she said. "But it was Mr. Plump . . . Mr. Pumpelly in his brown suit!"

Wendy still wasn't satisfied. "What about the moan in the attic?" she said. "How did you make that?"

"I told you chirrun to stay out of the attic," Mizriz Sawyer said.

Mr. Walker began to laugh. "It wasn't a moan," he explained. "It was a hoot . . . or rather a *whooo*. When I went up tonight to check and see if there were any cinders on the roof from the swamp fire, I discovered that Captain Horniblow had gotten trapped in the attic. I let him back out of the window before I put it down."

"What window?" Wendy said. "Not the garret window?"

"Yes, of course," Mr. Walker said. "It would have been awfully hot to sleep in that little garret room if that window didn't open."

"So that's how you got out!" Marc said to Snoad. Everyone got quiet.

"Well Wendy, you can say you saved a beast's life," Uncle Ed said.

"Me and Marc," Wendy insisted. "If he hadn't grabbed my dress . . ." She shivered to think about it.

"And don't forget about Wanda and Michael," said Uncle Ed. "If they hadn't come back across the canal to get me, we probably wouldn't have fished you or Snoad out."

"That's right," said Wendy. "They did go back when you called."

"Thank goodness some chirrun around here minds," Mizriz Sawyer said, then added, *"sometimes,* anyway."

Wendy smiled at her. She felt so bad that she had suspected her. She was a beauty — not a beast. And Mr. Pumpelly too, she thought, as he took a coverlet off the armchair and put it over a yawning Michael's shoulders.

"The water level decision is not due until tomorrow morning," Snoad said. "If Mr. Walker will take back the stolen report, I think I can get everything back in order for the closing on your land tomorrow afternoon," he said to Uncle Ed.

Wendy looked at her uncle. He just stared at Snoad. He didn't look happy at his offer. Finally he spoke. "All right," he said. "We'll close."

Wendy jumped off the sofa. She gave Uncle Ed a big kiss. It left a circle of crumbs on his cheek. He smiled and brushed them away.

"Then we can come back and close our wedding

vows," Allison said.

Snoad's face turned red. "Oh, that's right! We never even got to get married!" Then he looked up at her with that same sad, brown look Wendy had seen earlier. "Are you sure you want to marry a . . . a beast?" he said.

Allison smiled at him. "You need someone to tame you," she said.

Everyone laughed.

Wendy felt wonderful. She was wet and tired but she was going to live at Somerset!

Michael yawned a gigantic yawn and laid his head on the arm of the sofa and closed his eyes.

Wendy looked at the cake sitting on the table in front of them. "Can I have another piece?" she asked.

Mizriz Sawyer took the knife and started carving the basement from what was left of the house. Then she stopped, and moved the knife to the edge of the cake and sliced off a big chunk of lake and green land. She put it on a plate and handed it to Wendy.

"Welcome to Somerset!" she said.

Wendy smiled at her and then at Uncle Ed, and finally at Mr. Snoad. "Did you know that I read that they call this place the haunt of beasts?" she said.

Michael yawned again and opened one eye. *"I believe it!"* he mumbled, and everyone laughed — Wendy the loudest of all.

About the author . . .

Carole Marsh, a native of Atlanta, Georgia, owns and operates Marsh Media Methods, a communications consulting firm with offices in Rocky Mount and Tryon, North Carolina.

She was named 1979 Communicator of the Year by the Carolinas Association of Business Communicators and has received numerous awards for her writing and photography.

Currently Ms. Marsh edits an employee magazine for Hardee's Food Systems that goes to 13,000 readers in 37 states and several foreign countries. A 76-page, 4-color quality of life Chamber of Commerce magazine she recently produced scored 99 out of a possible 99 in national Chamber competition. Ms. Marsh's articles and photographs have been published in various newspapers, corporate publications and business magazines.

Ms. Marsh's interest in history and historic preservation led her to write juvenile mysteries emphasizing both subjects. She has a daughter, Michele, 14, and a son, Michael, 8. Her first juvenile mystery, *The Missing Head Mystery,* published in 1979, was featured in a film shown at the American Library Association's annual meeting in New York. The book was also nominated for the American Association of University Women's juvenile fiction award.

Ms. Marsh is currently living in Tryon, North Carolina, and working on *The Mystery of the Lost Colony*$_{TM}$ and *The Mystery of the World's Fair*$_{TM}$.

THE SOMERSET PLACE characters in the photographs, left to right: Wanda Simpson, age 9, lives in Columbia, North Carolina. Michael Marsh, age 8, lives in Tryon, North Carolina, and is the author's son. Marc Snapp, age 9, lives in Creswell, North Carolina, where Somerset Place is located. Wendy Longmeyer, age 13, lives in Greenville, South Carolina.

HISTORY MYSTERY™

HISTORY MYSTERY™ books are published exclusively by Gallopade Publishing Group. This unique concept of combining historic fact and contemporary fiction was developed for readers at the age they typically study their area of the country's history in school. The geographic locations and physical places featured in each book exist today, so that children may actually visit these historic sites after reading the related book. Many of the "real" children portraying the books' characters in the photographs live near the general historic area highlighted.

It is Gallopade Publishing Group's sincerest hope that our HISTORY MYSTERY™ series will instill an enthusiasm for history and a belief in historic preservation in our young people — particularly since they are the future guardians of both.

Gallopade Publishing Group series and titles in print or to be published:

HISTORY MYSTERY™ BOOKS

The Historic Albemarle, North Carolina, Mystery Series
    The Missing Head Mystery by Carole Marsh
    The Secret of Somerset Place by Carole Marsh
    The Mystery of the Lost Colony by Carole Marsh
The Historic Blue Ridge, North Carolina, Mystery Series
The Historic Low Country, South Carolina, Mystery Series
The Historic Highland, South Carolina, Mystery Series
The Historic Georgia Mystery Series
The Historic Virginias Mystery Series
The Historic Tennessee Mystery Series
The Historic Kentucky Mystery Series
The Historic New England Mystery Series

REAL PEOPLE/REAL PLACES™ BOOKS

The Mystery of the World's Fair by Carole Marsh
The Mystery of New York City
The Big Atlanta Mystery
The Dizzy Disney World Mystery
The Kentucky Derby Mystery
The Wacky Williamsburg Mystery

TEACHERS & LIBRARIANS:
Media Kits are available for each title. Contact the publisher about these, as well as visits by book authors and book "characters."

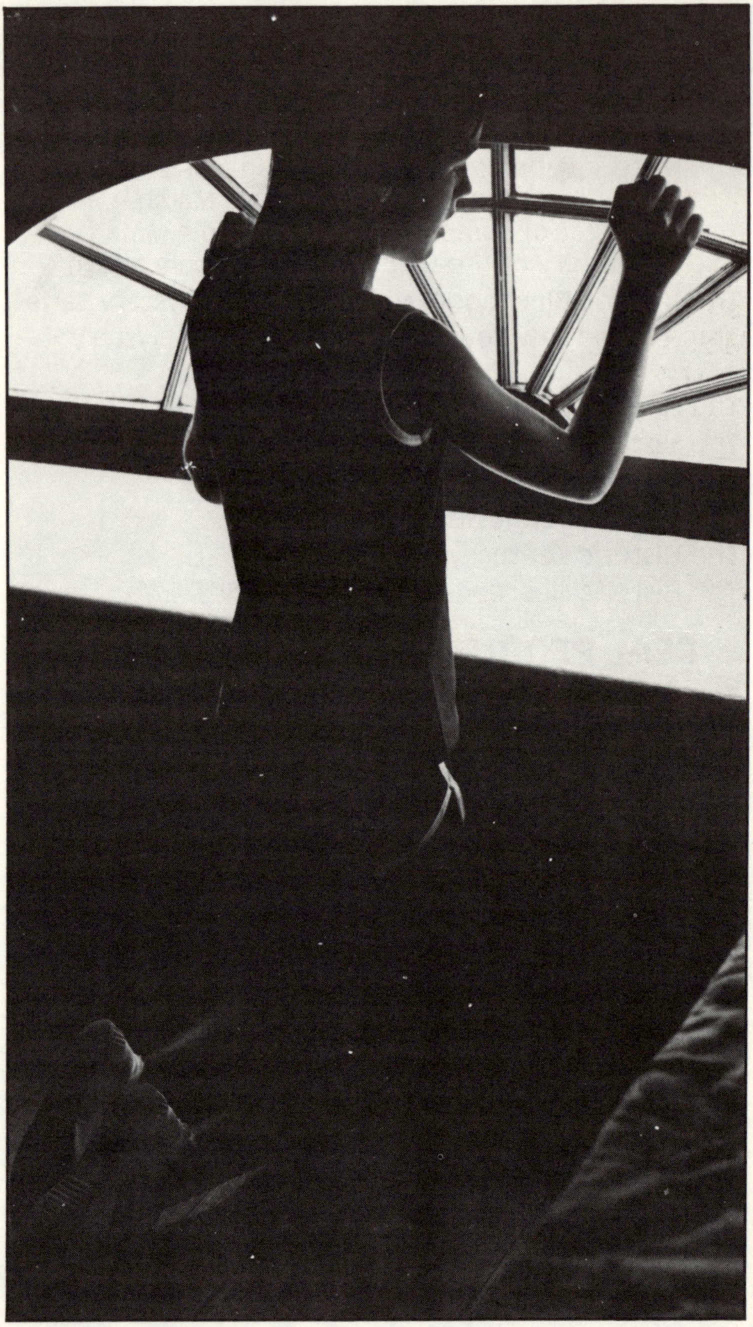

Dear Reader,

If you enjoyed this book, I hope you will order other HISTORY MISTERY₮ₘ books in the Historic Albemarle, North Carolina Mystery Series. When you place an order, we will add your name to "The Mystery Messenger" mailing list. This is a newsletter published just for HISTORY MYSTERY₮ₘ fans.

Happy reading!

Carole Marsh

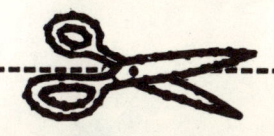

Dear Ms. Marsh,

I really did like this book! Please add my name to "The Mystery Messenger" newsletter mailing list. I would also like to order the following:

☐ The Missing Head Mystery
☐ The Secret of Somerset Place
☐ The Mystery of the Lost Colony
☐ The Mystery of the World's Fair

Enclosed is $3.95 for each book, plus 16¢ tax for each book (only if I live in North Carolina) and $1.00 for postage and handling for each book.

Hurry, please! Thank you.

My name is _____

My address is _____
              STREET   CITY/STATE   ZIP

The school I attend is _____

Mail to: Gallopade Publishing Group
P.O. Box 469/Rocky Mount, NC 27801

Dear Ms. Marsh,

I really did like this book! Please add my name to "The Mystery Messenger" newsletter mailing list. I would also like to order the following:

☐ The Missing Head Mystery
☐ The Secret of Somerset Place
☐ The Mystery of the Lost Colony
☐ The Mystery of the World's Fair

Enclosed is $3.95 for each book, plus 16¢ tax for each book (only if I live in North Carolina) and $1.00 for postage and handling for each book.

Hurry, please! Thank you.

My name is _____

My address is _____
STREET   CITY/STATE   ZIP

The school I attend is _____

Mail to: Gallopade Publishing Group
P.O. Box 469/Rocky Mount, NC 27801

Dear Ms. Marsh,

I really did like this book! Please add my name to "The Mystery Messenger" newsletter mailing list. I would also like to order the following:

☐ The Missing Head Mystery
☐ The Secret of Somerset Place
☐ The Mystery of the Lost Colony
☐ The Mystery of the World's Fair

Enclosed is $3.95 for each book, plus 16¢ tax for each book (only if I live in North Carolina) and $1.00 for postage and handling for each book.

Hurry, please! Thank you.

My name is _____

My address is _____
STREET   CITY/STATE   ZIP

The school I attend is _____

Mail to: Gallopade Publishing Group
P.O. Box 469/Rocky Mount, NC 27801